DREAMS FROM THE ENDZ

DREAMS
FROM THE ENDZ

Faïza Guène

Translated from the French
by Sarah Ardizzone

Chatto & Windus
LONDON

Published by Chatto & Windus 2008

First published in France in 2006 by Hachette Littératures
under the title *Du rêve pour les oufs*

2 4 6 8 10 9 7 5 3 1

Copyright © Hachette Littératures, 2006
Translation copyright © Sarah Ardizzone 2008

Faïza Guène has asserted her right under the Copyright, Designs
and Patents Act 1988 to be identified as the author of this work

First published in Great Britain in 2008 by Chatto & Windus
Random House, 20 Vauxhall Bridge Road, London SW1V 2SA
www.rbooks.co.uk

Addresses for companies within The Random House Group Limited
can be found at: www.randomhouse.co.uk/offices.htm

The Random House Group Limited Reg. No. 954009

A CIP catalogue record for this book is available from the British Library

ISBN 9780701181543

The Random House Group Limited supports The Forest Stewardship Council (FSC),
the leading international forest certification organisation.
All our titles that are printed on Greenpeace approved FSC certified paper carry the
FSC logo. Our paper procurement policy can be found at
www.rbooks.co.uk/environment

Mixed Sources
Product group from well-managed
forests and other controlled sources
www.fsc.org Cert no. TT-COC-2139
© 1996 Forest Stewardship Council

FSC

Set in New Baskerville by Palimpsest Book Production Limited,
Grangemouth, Stirlingshire

Printed and bound in the UK by
CPI Mackays, Chatham ME5 8TD

This book has been selected to receive financial assistance from
English PEN's Writers in Translation programme supported by Bloomberg.

This book is supported by the French Ministry of Foreign Affairs as part of the Burgess
programme run by the Cultural Department of the French Embassy in London.
(www.frenchbooknews.com)

Liberté • Égalité • Fraternité
RÉPUBLIQUE FRANÇAISE

Contents

The Chill of the City

It's freezing in this *bled*, the wind makes my eyes
stream, and I'm legging it to keep warm. Wrong place
to live, is what I'm thinking, the climate's not right,
because deep down it's just a question of climate,
and this morning the crazy cold of France is paralysing
me.

I'm Ahlème, by the way, and I'm walking through
the crush of all these people in a rush, bumping into
each other, running late, arguing, on their mobiles,
not smiling, and I can see my brothers who are so
cold, like me. I can always spot them, it's something
in their eyes, like they want to be invisible, or somewhere else. But they're here.

I never complain at home, not even when our
heating cuts out, because Dad just goes: 'You keep
quiet now, you didn't live through the winter of
'63.' Not much I can say to that, in 1963 I wasn't
even born. So I shuffle and slide along France's
slippery streets, passing Rue Joubert where a few
prostitutes on the pavements call out to each other.
They look like beat-up old dolls who aren't afraid

1

of the cold any more. Working girls are the climatic exception, it doesn't matter where they are, they've stopped feeling anything.

My appointment with the temping agency is for 10.40 a.m. Not 45. Not 30. Things are kind of precise here in France, where every minute counts, and it's something I'll never get used to. I was born on the other side of the sea, and the African minute contains a lot more than sixty seconds.

Mr Miloudi, the youth adviser in my area, suggested I apply to this new outfit: Temp Plus.

Miloudi's old skool. He's been running the youth advisory service on Uprising Estate since back in the day, and he's seen all the ASBOs in our endz. He's efficient, I guess. But he's always in a hurry. So it wasn't like there was any hanging around in my interview:

'Sit down, young lady . . .'

'Thank you.'

'And next time, please remember to knock before entering.'

'Sorry, I wasn't thinking.'

'I'm only saying it for your own benefit, you can fail an interview for that kind of thing.'

'I'll remember.'

'Good, let's get going, no time to waste, we've only got a twenty-minute slot. You need to fill out the skills form in front of you, write in block capitals in the boxes, and don't make any spelling mistakes. If you're not sure about a word, ask me for the dictionary. Did you bring your CV?'

2

'Yes. Five copies, like you said.'

'Very good. There's the form, fill it out carefully. I'll be back in five minutes.'

He took a box of kitchen matches out of his pocket, together with a pack of Marlboros, and walked away, leaving me to face my destiny. There were piles of files on his desk, forms everywhere I looked, taking up all the space. And a giant clock fixed to the wall. Each time its hands moved, it made a noise that echoed in my ears like someone ringing the end of time. I felt hot all of a sudden. Mental block. The five minutes sped by like a TGV, and all I'd written was my surname, my first name and my date of birth.

I could hear Mr Miloudi's dry cough in the corridor; he was coming back.

'So? Where are you up to? Have you finished?'

'No. Not yet.'

'But you haven't filled in *anything*!' he complained, leaning over the piece of paper.

'I didn't get time.'

'There are plenty of people waiting for an appointment, I have other clients after you, as you saw in the waiting room. We've only got ten minutes to contact the SREP now, because at this time of year there's no point going via AGPA, there won't be any places left. I suggest we try for paid training at the FAJ . . . Why can't you fill it out? It's straightforward enough.'

'I don't know what to put in the "life plans" box . . .'

'You must have some idea.'

'No.'

'I can see from your CV that you've had plenty of

professional experience, there must be something there you enjoyed.'

'Those were casual jobs, like being a waitress or a shop assistant. They were about money, Mr Miloudi, not my life plan.'

'OK, let's leave the application form for now, we haven't got time. I'm going to give you the address of another temping agency, while we're waiting to hear from the FAJ.'

Johanna at Temp Plus looks sixteen, her voice trembles and it's painful trying to make out what she's saying. I get that she's asking me to fill out a questionnaire. She gives me a biro with her office's stupid logo on it and asks me to follow her. She's wearing these extra-stretchy jeans that show up all the times she's stuffed her face instead of sticking to her Weight Watchers' diet – they make her look like she's having an affair or something. She points to a seat by a small table where I'm meant to sit down. It's difficult to write, my fingers are frozen stiff, I'm finding it hard to unclench them. It reminds me of when Dad – the Boss, we call him – used to come home from work. He always needed a bit of time before he could open his hands. 'It's because of the pneumatic drill,' he used to say.

I scribble, I fill in their boxes, I tick and sign. Everything on their application form is teeny-tiny and their questions are bordering on the annoying. No, I'm not married, no I haven't got any kids, or a driving licence, no I didn't go on to higher education, no I'm not registered disabled and no I'm not French. In fact, where's the box for: 'My life's FLOPPED'? That way, I'll just tick it, end of story.

Johanna, whose jeans are so tight they're cutting up into her crotch, puts on this sympathetic voice and offers me my first temping 'assignment'. It's funny how they call them 'assignments'. Makes shitty jobs seem like an adventure.

She's offering me stocktaking out in Leroy Merlin next Friday evening. I say yes, straight up, I need the work so badly I'd take almost anything.

I come out of there feeling well pleased with myself, which just goes to show it doesn't take much.

Then I head off to join Linda and Nawel at the Cour de Rome, which is a café in the Saint-Lazare area, near to the agency. They've been trying to see me for a few weeks now, but to be honest I mostly avoid going out when I haven't got any money. Plus these days they're glued to their boyfriends, which is kind of boring, and I always feel so clumsy plonked in between them. I'm not far off winning the European and African Championships for Best Female Gooseberry.

The girls are sitting on the bench at the back of the café. Typical, bunch of smokers hiding away, I know their old tricks by heart. They even set up this HQ in our endz where they used to hang out behind the stadium, to bill up one, and the code to meet was: 'Anyone fancy keeping fit?'

They're dressed to kill, nothing new there. I've noticed how slick they always look, and I'm thinking how can they spend so much time getting dressed, doing their hair and make-up? Nothing's left to chance, everything matches, it's all calculated and chosen carefully.

It's not often I sign up to making the effort, but when I do it nearly kills me, it's too much like hard work if you ask me. What wouldn't us girls do for an admiring look or a compliment on a bad-hair day? So if someone says she's gone all out with the garms just to please herself it's like, yeah right!

I'm level with the girls now and they light their cigarettes in sync, welcoming me with a warm smoky 'hi'.

Sticking to the rules, a 'wassup?' follows hot on its heels, and we always leave a bit of space to think about this before kicking off the discussion.

Then comes the question I've been dreading.

'Any new boyfriends to tell us about?' A shake of the head, they get the idea. How come they always ask about boyfriends, plural? I mean, it's hard enough finding one person you like, so why complicate things?

Next up, same old: 'So what's a *fine* girl like you doing still single? Your problem is, you don't really want a boyfriend . . . You've only got yourself to blame, you're too choosy. We've set you up with some fit guys, we're talking bare buff beasts for real, there's nothing else we can do for you, you're shut off.'

I can never get them to understand it's not as bad as they're making out because, if things work out, it's not like I'll be going through the menopause tomorrow. But they just keep on busting a gut to introduce me to total plonkers. We're talking guys with an IQ of 2 who are so up themselves it's unreal, or else complete tossers, or wastemans who can't string two words together, or manic depressives.

So, I do this nifty manoeuvre to get them to change the subject – I've got a real talent for dodging obstacles and problems, three times African and European champion.

Basically, I reckon the girls have already decided on their life plan, same as most people, it's all mapped out in their heads, like pieces of a jigsaw waiting to fit together. They divide their time between their J.O.B. and leisure, they go on holiday to the same place every summer, they always buy the same brand of deodorant, their families are chilled and they've got long-term boyfriends. In fact, even their guys are spotless, I mean, I like them and everything, but you wouldn't catch me going away with them for a weekend. No flies there. Plus they come from the same village as the girls, back in the *bled*, so their parents are bare haps. It's like incest is back in fashion. At least if it's your brother, you can be sure he comes from exactly the same place as you, just ask your mum. The girls reckon it's practical, because if the families came from different traditions, they wouldn't agree on everything; and another thing, it makes bringing up the kids more complicated if you don't speak the same language . . . If you ask me, they're just stupid details, and you don't set up home together just because it's practical.

Nawel's back from holiday; she was in Algeria staying with her dad's family, and I tell her she's lost loads of weight, at least five kilos.

'Yeah? Am I really skinny?'

'You've dried up, for real. People'll feel sorry for you, *miskina*!'

'That's going back to the *bled* for you.'

'Diet holiday, innit.'

'Yeah, for real . . . All that heat, stringy beans every meal, your gran's jokes, Chilean soap operas . . . Course you're gonna lose weight.'

'How did you do it?' asks Linda, she's curious now. 'Two whole months in the *bled*, I'd have got depressed, straight up.'

'I guess the time just goes. But the TV, man, that was ova-wack, there's only one channel. Even *Mr Bean* is censored over there.'

'At least you don't get embarrassing stuff like the whole tribe in front of the telly and bam! a hot scene flashes up, or one of those shower gel ads. You get me, the old man starts coughing and you've got to grab that remote and zap, fast as. That's why we've got a satellite dish round ours now. It's saved our lives because on French TV they RATE all the girls getting their kit off, and it's like totally random.'

'How was it staying with your family?'

'Bunch of scavengers more like . . . The first week, they loved us up because our suitcases were bulging. But as soon as we'd handed out all the presents that was it, our ratings dropped. I said to my mum: "Next summer, I swear on the Koran, let's just get Tati to sponsor us, it'd make life a lot easier."'

Coming up, it's time for the neighbourhood gossip

with Linda.com. She's too much, this girl, a total blab-
bermouth. Linda knows everything about everybody,
I don't get how she does it, sometimes she even knows
what's going on with people before they do.

'You know Tony Lopez . . . ?'

'No, who's he?'

'Yes you do, the new guy at number 16.'

'The blond one?'

'Nah, tall guy with brown hair. Works at Midas.'

'Yeah, what about him?'

'He's going out with Gwendolyn!'

'What, that short girl? The redhead in your block?'

'No, not her. The anorexic with loads of half-
finished tattoos. Nawel, you know who I mean . . .'

'Yeah, got you, I see her on the bus on the way to
my J.O.B. So how come she never got her tattoos
finished? I've always wondered about that.'

'How's Linda supposed to know that?' I ask, me
being naive.

'Yeah, yeah, I know this one . . .'

'Shit, man, you've got all the tabloid. Spit it out.'

'So, she was with this dodgy guy before, right, a
tattoo artist. Well, that's it, innit. He starts on her
tattoos and then he never gets to finish them because
he dumps her for another girl.'

'Bastard. He could of finished the job.'

'So anyway, Anorexia's going out with Tony Lopez,
and then what?'

'Well, he wanted to leave her. According to my
sources, it's because he's sticking it in the accountant
round at Midas. But seeing as Gwendolyn ova-LIKES

9

him, she did all this psychological pressure shit to make him stay. So that's what he ended up doing and then he had to pay for it big time . . .'

'Meaning? Spit it out! Cut the tacky suspense.'

'Wifey only goes and makes a kid behind his back. Like, she's preggo out to *here*. Crazy, innit?'

Every time, Linda signs off with: 'Crazy, innit?'

Before going our separate ways, we told each other a few more stories, the kind you tell in hushed voices, and the same smile that gave away a few of our secrets is protecting me now against the big chill of the outside world.

The platform's black with people, *severe delays occurring*. One train in four, that's what they said on the radio.

No choice, I'm gripping the overhead bar in the carriage. No air in this RER, people are pushing me, crushing me. The train is sweating and I'm feeling choked by all these sad bodies craving colour. All the air in Africa wouldn't be enough for them. They're ghosts, and they're all sick, contaminated with sadness.

I head back to Ivry to help my neighbour, Auntie Mariatou, and her children. My asthmatic RER spits me out into our endz, where it's even colder. Days like today, you don't know where you're going any more, you're clean out of luck, too bad, I guess. Yeah, it's sad, but luckily, deep down, there's still this little thing that helps you get up in the morning. There's no guarantee, but you hold out for it getting better one day. Like Auntie says: 'The best stories have the worst beginnings.'

The Dollar Tree

The children in this house don't know how lucky they are. It's like a poem, the way their family surrounds them with so much love and warmth. And Auntie Mariatou is the mother in all her splendour, who harvests the best from the cotton plant to cosset her children, she's the spirit of tenderness. What fascinates me is seeing her bring them up so strictly, while bathing them in honey at the same time. I get fired up when I talk about her, because she's who I'd like to be one day. She's my role model as a woman, a mother and a wife. Auntie is very beautiful, her lips are juicy, her hips are wide and back in the day her curves set more than one man in the village dreaming. She's got a full figure, but she's so natural she treads as lightly as an antelope – she's got a certain '*je ne sais quoi*', as they say in my host country, that could make size 0 models tremble.

She and her husband, Papa Demba, have four beautiful children. They're like Russian dolls, the way they all follow on from each other, and they look like each other too. Wandé is the oldest, and she's eight. Today, I've come round to help her with her homework. She wants to be a singer, and complains that none of the *toubabs* in her class will be her boyfriend because she's got hair extensions. Next up are the twins, Issa and Moussa. They're so smart, those two, and they freak people out because they can make you believe anything. As for the last one, all he can do right now is bawl, he's only six months old. He's my pride, this little one. It was me who whispered his name to Auntie Mariatou, when she was big on pregnancy and short on ideas. I chose Amady because it's the name of the first boy I fell in love with. I was crazy about him. He was always dragging me on to the roundabout in the kids' play-ground and then he'd push us off as hard as he could. We'd be going so fast my pleated skirt would fly up, and I couldn't hold it down because I was clinging on to the bars, too scared of getting my face smashed in to let go.

Amady was so cheeky, he was always using that trick to get a peek under my skirt. I didn't click until much later, I can only have been about five at the time.

While we're on the subject of baby Amady, one day when Auntie was pushing his pram in the park, she got stopped by an old gypsy woman, the one everyone reckons is mad. This gypsy said Amady would grow up to be an exceptional man who would make a permanent mark on History, and he'd do something very important that would take everybody by surprise. She said the baby carried the hopes of a nation in its belly.

Of course, same as most people around here, Auntie Mariatou didn't take her seriously. She even laughed about it while she was changing her son's nappy.

'If all the hopes this little one carries in his belly come out as poo, then his people haven't got off to a great start, have they?'

I'm curious about this old gypsy, even if everybody says she's crazy and just scares little kids. Sometimes I find myself watching her, from a distance. In the mornings, she goes out for a walk on her own, a big black shawl over her shoulders, and now and then she stops to feed the birds. To be honest, she scares the shit out of me, especially when I see her talking to the pigeons. She'll catch one of them, always the biggest one. Then, she'll settle it on her hand, and it's strange because each time it's like the bird is tame and it doesn't even try to fly away. So she starts whispering things to it. From a way off, you'd think the bird was answering her, that they're having a conversation and it's the most normal thing in the world. This goes on for a while and then, all of a sudden, she'll let out a horrible high-pitched shriek and all the birds she invited to the feast of breadcrumbs fly off in every direction. They take off like crazies. It's anarchy in the grey sky of Ivry.

When everything calms down again, and those wings are flapping further off, you notice something weird. The old lady's still there, standing stiff, and in the hollow of her hand, close to her mouth, the big fat pigeon has stayed on, calm as you like. She heads off with the bird eventually, like it's no big deal, and the stingy pigeons wait for the old lady to leave so they can come back, one by one, for their dessert.

Sometimes, I imagine what happens next: she wrings the bird's neck and then takes a bite, sinking her canines like a hungry wolf. She ends up swallowing the whole thing raw, feathers, head and beak.

I'm really curious about this old lady. I couldn't say how old she is, or what era she's from. It's like she's outside of time.

I'm sitting on a wooden chair in the middle of the living room, waiting impatiently for today's fix of *Star Academy* to finish so that Wandé and I can get on with her homework. It's impossible to separate her from the screen, she's stuck to it like a cockroach on a Baygon strip. I think it's because she's in love with one of the contestants, the short blond guy who got through to the final. She reminds me of my little brother Foued, on his PlayStation, when he's in the middle of a shoot-em-up.

'Wandé! It's already half past seven, sunshine! I'm not waiting up all night for you to do your homework.'

'But it's the final.'

'Look, I'm going home soon. So either you turn the telly off now, or you can do your homework on your own.'

'I wouldn't bother, Ahlème! She'll just have to get a zero.'

'Shhh, Mum! I can't hear!'

'I beg your pardon! Who are you telling to *shhhh*, you badly brought up child!?'

'She's got a date with her future husband,' I say, teasing Wandé. 'He's about to sing.'

Auntie Mariatou is furious, and pulls out the TV plug.

'There *are* more important things than television, you know! This kid would wet herself rather than miss a crumb of that programme, and it's getting out of hand!'

Wandé puts on this sulky face that totally suits her. Ever since she got cane-rows it makes her look funny when she sulks. Her face is pulled back and taut. Cane-rows are the African facelift. Auntie Mariatou always pulls too hard – I should know, she does my hair sometimes too. She gets good results, but she yanks your head like it's a carpet and this can go on for hours. It helps if you grit your teeth. Then again, she knows what she's doing, it's her job, and as the Boss would say, you should never argue with someone who's working. Some customers come from far away for Auntie to do their hair, because she's got a steady hand and knows all about fashion – what people like, what works.

Recently, she's subscribed to an American magazine for Afro hairstyles. She says that black women in America are up for taking risks with their hair, they'll try even the craziest stuff. They reveal the secrets of stars like Mary J. Blige and Alicia Keys in that magazine.

Auntie's funny when she talks about it, she gets carried away.

'Oh per-leeze! Take that Beyoncé girl who waddles around in those MTV videos, you didn't seriously think she was born with straight blonde silky hair, did you? Her hair's as frizzy as mine, sweetheart, she's just got the means to make everybody forget, that's all.'

Auntie Mariatou works four days a week at Afro Star 2000, a hairdressing salon in Château d'Eau, Paris proper. She's made a lot of good friends from the heads she styles, most of them women from the Ivory Coast.

Auntie loves hairdressing, it's been her passion for the longest time. Her secret ambition is to set herself up over in America, and open a big salon.

'Too bad if I can't speak English, I'll just talk the language of hair.'

Her dream of America goes back to her childhood, when the skin on her face was pulled too tight by the plaits her mum gave her. While everybody was talking about Paris, she had her sights set on New York. Sometimes she says that if she hadn't followed her husband, Papa Demba, to France for love, she'd definitely have gone over there to hook up with I don't know which distant cousin.

Auntie Mariatou used to live in Senegal, in Mbacké, and when it was time for the American soap on telly, the whole neighbourhood would gather in front of this tiny set that was fixed up in the middle of the courtyard. It was like a religious ritual. When it was sunny, someone would get up and put a palm leaf above the screen.

Sometimes the picture would go fuzzy or the worn-out television would go totally blank for a minute or two. This was an eternity for a little girl with tears in her eyes, and she would start cursing everything imaginable until one of the spectators got up to mend the set. As often as not, it was her cousin Yahia, nicknamed Romeo in the village because he flirted with all the girls behind their parents' backs. He would go and find a nice stainless-steel fork to stick in the bumhole of that TV with a mind of its own. The same fork, by the way, that had been used a few days earlier to calm little Aminata's tetanus attack.

The Mr Fix-It approach always worked a treat and got a speedy result: the picture was back faster than you could say DIY and the gathering would let out a relieved 'aaah . . .'. Mariatou always made sure she sat in the front row, for the best seat. Her mouth wide open, mesmerised by what she was watching, she would concentrate so hard she didn't even bother shaking off the flies that settled on her face or tickled her bare dry feet.

Her cousin Yahia, AKA Romeo, the one who stuck the fork in the TV, thought the little girl's fascination for the big country beyond the ocean was kind of funny, so he took her out in a boat to play a trick on her. He told her this story that she swallowed, hook, line and sinker: The Tale of the Dollar Tree.

'According to legend, there are some extraordinary

trees in America. These magical trees sprout notes, dollar bills, instead of leaves. They can grow in all kinds of conditions and throughout the year, because they don't need water to quench their thirst. Everybody has the right to benefit from the trees over there, which is why they're a people who know neither hunger nor thirst.'

Mariatou dreamt about the Dollar Tree from morning till night until she reached the age of reason.

I think she still believes in it a bit, I think we all did once upon a time. The Boss was convinced that all you had to do was dig the ground in France to make your fortune. When he tells us that, it makes me feel sick, but I smile anyway.

Standing Proud

'Are you all right, Dad?'

'It's cold in here. I've only got five cigarettes left, you know, for the whole evening.'

'It's because they cut the heating off, I told you yesterday, they'll connect us up again sometime this week. As for your cigarettes, I'll get you some from the shop, it doesn't close till late.'

'Did you just pop out?'

'I've been out since this morning.'

'Really? I didn't hear you go.'

'By the way, Dad, have you heard about Michel, the neighbour from downstairs?'

'The one with a missing arm?'

'No, the other one.'

'Which other one? The thin guy who's always getting yelled at by that ugly-as-sin wife of his?'

'No, the fat one with glasses, the same guy whose dog died last year.'

'What's the matter with him?'

'They're saying he tried to commit suicide.'

'Again?'

'Yes, it's the third – no, the fourth time, I think.'

'The fourth, already! My God, how time flies . . . Is he dead?'

'No, he messed up again, he's in hospital.'

'I always told you he was a complete waste of space! And he can't even kill himself? I mean, dying isn't exactly hard.'

'If you say so.'

'I've only got five cigarettes left, you know, for –'

'Yes, I know, I'll pop down and get some for you. Where's Foued, Dad?'

'Playing football outside with the kids.'

'Right, I'm going to get him, he's meant to be home by now, you know that, it's half past ten –'

'Half past ten? It's late, the shop'll be shutting . . .'

He's always like that, the Boss, but it feels like he's worse right now. It's since the accident – it'll be three years next month. Three years isn't long, but when you see him like this, saying stuff that doesn't make any sense, sitting in his armchair all day, in his pyjamas, you'd think he'd always been that way. He spends all his time in front of the TV now, it's turned into this fully signed-up member of the family. Telly rules the Boss's new life, he doesn't need a watch any more. *Télé Matin* means it's coffee time, the news means time for lunch, *Inspector Derrick* means time for an after-noon nap, and the play-out music on the evening film means time for bed. He falls asleep and the next day the same ritual starts up all over again. ~~Ever since he~~ went AWOL, he's been living a never-ending day.

I remember, it happened very early in the morning, he was working on the building site, and he was balancing high up just like he'd balanced his whole life.

Except that day, he wasn't wearing a hard hat. Dad had given his hat to Fernandes – the one who doesn't touch booze – because he was strolling about under the beams and Dad reckoned it was dangerous. Knowing him, the Boss probably thought: 'I'm up there, there's no risk of anything falling on my head apart from lightning.'

Nobody really knows why, but he fell off that god-forsaken girder. The fall was so spectacular, none of the guys thought he'd ever get up again. In fact, his body didn't do so badly, two or three broken bones and a stupid strained ankle.

But his head hit the joist when he tipped over, and because of the blow he can't think straight any more.

Seeing as he wasn't wearing a helmet, the contractor refused to pay damages. So first we had the workers' union, then the legal system, the lawyer, the trial. Luckily, we won the case in the end. His disability was recognised, unfit for work. So he can draw a pension and he even gets a free travel pass.

But I remember how us and the lawyer, we had a real battle on our hands, waving papers in every direction, medical reports, statements from this person and that.

It was tough to start with, but we just got on with it.

21

For the first few months after the accident, there were mornings in the week when Dad would wake up at four o'clock, like everything was normal again, he'd wash, pray, pack up his billycan and get ready to go. I don't think there was any logic to the order he did those things in, by the way. As soon as I realised he was up and about, I'd have to get out of bed and explain that he wasn't going to work after all and that made me feel kind of sick because he would reply, sounding all confused: 'Yes, of course, you're right, I'd forgotten, today's Sunday.'

Foued doesn't like me coming to get him when he's out with his bredrins, he says I'm shaming him because he's a *man dem* now, you get me. Mostly, I avoid doing it, but I warned him about tonight and I've noticed that he's started disrespecting the rules I set at home. He's just a kid after all, he's only fifteen. He has to get up early for school tomorrow, and there's no reason for him to be outside at this time.

I bet he's on the other side of the estate, at the Pierre de Coubertin Stadium. I've noticed how most sports grounds get to be called Pierre de Coubertin. How unoriginal is that? If you ask me, we should rename our stadium Ladji Doucouré one of these days.

Anyway, the stadium's at the foot of what everyone calls 'the Hill', it's like a big mound looming over these endz. So I position myself up on the top, and I get this amazing view. The lights are coming at me from all around and it's beautiful.

I'm surrounded by all these screwball housing

blocks that hem in our lives here, our noises and smells. I'm standing alone, in the middle of their wacky architecture, their garish colours, their mad shapes that have cradled our illusions for so long. The days are over when running water and electricity were enough to camouflage the injustices, and the shanty towns are far away. I'm standing proud and thinking about a whole heap of stuff. What's happened in our endz these past few weeks has stirred up the world press, but after a few clashes between youths and the police, everything's calmed down again. What can the carcasses of burnt-out cars do to change anything, when an army of fanatics is trying to silence us?

The only legitimate curfew is the one I'm imposing this evening, as a non-French citizen, on my fifteen-year-old little brother.

I can see Foued down below, in the middle of the stadium, dodging around with, it's got to be said, a lot of skill. He's playing with ten other boys from the neighbourhood, all roughly the same age. I know most of them, I've watched some of them grow up. Even the two Villovitch brothers are there. I haven't seen that pair of wastemans for the longest time. They've been avoiding me since our last encounter. They were so embarrassed, they'd have vanished like fog if they could.

That evening, I'd gone down to the basement to lock up Foued's bike. I pushed open the reinforced door with the front wheel, because sometimes it jams, and that's when I surprised these two tossers. They were sitting on this old two-seater sofa that got retired to the basement years ago, and they had their backs to me, so at first they didn't realise I'd invaded their privacy.

In front of me was the smart device they'd rigged up. Thanks to an illegal power socket, they'd set up a small television on an up-ended box, and installed a PlayStation on top as their DVD player. It was this comic scene where all I could see were the parts of their bodies that weren't hidden by the sofa, meaning their sweaty little necks and their right arms furiously jiggling about.

Centre stage was an unofficial episode of the Olympic Games. On the screen, a busty blonde was giving a breathtaking performance of rhythmic gymnastics, supported a bit too closely by the guys on the parallel bars. The basement had been transformed into a projection room for bimbo-trash.

> *Oh Puberty, I write your name.*
> *On the Concrete, I write your name.*

I decided not to laugh when it came to their big moment. I didn't want to risk castrating such virile young specimens and being held responsible for their future 'issues'. Then came the inevitable 'mmm . . . mmm' – it was time to stop the show, I needed to put the bike away.

I'll never forget the expressions on their faces. They were caught with their hands in the till, so to speak. It nearly killed me trying to keep a straight face as I locked the bike up.

The tossers didn't dare turn their heads my way,

they just cleared up their gear, hot with shame. I exited the cave of Ali Baba and the Forty Wankers, leaving those two to their guilt so I could finally let out my choked-up laughter in the lift. I nearly went back down to thank them afterwards, I hadn't laughed like that for ages. So, that's why the little shits have been avoiding me.

I make my entrance on the pitch and my budding Zizou of a brother is already staring me down. He's after my skin for being on his territory.

What happened to respect for elders? I'll drag him home by the elastic on his boxers, if that's what it takes. Who does he think he is? I brought him up, this kid, and he may have a short memory span but I certainly don't. He owes me obedience. Just because he's cancelled his contract with Pampers, doesn't mean he can give me a hard time.

'Foued! You're coming home right now!'

'One last game and I'll be back. You go, it's cool.'

'Don't argue! I told you, we're leaving.'

''Low it, man! You're getting me vexed. I'm just coming.'

'You'd better shut it now! Who do you think you're talking to? You want to play it big in front of your bredrins? Well, you've flopped, little bro. Get your ass over here!'

He breaks off his fancy footwork, fuming, dead still now. Suddenly, there's this group hush thing. We're about twenty metres apart, both standing tall, and it's a battle of stares. Like in a western,

This Town Ain't Big Enough for the Both of Us or something.

To my amazement, one of the Villovitch brothers has the nerve to speak out at this key moment in the film.

'Let him play the last game, please, you can't do this to him.'

'As for you, Mr Masturbator, I don't remember anyone asking your opinion. You're the last person to tell me what I can or can't do . . .'

Miniprick lowers his head, humiliated. I'll be honest, I was a bit harsh. But those filthy kids wanted to seize the power. When you're the victim of a *coup d'état*, you've got to stand your ground.

Foued follows me without a word, he's too embarrassed to say 'bye to his bredrins. If he had a gun instead of eyes right now, there'd already be a bullet in my back. It's not like I need to say it, he knows: Rule Number One, Dad can never be left alone at home. Sometimes, I get the feeling I was born to look after other people. Foued is young, and he's not to blame for all this, but he's got to understand that he can't just do whatever he likes. He's at that age where he's got to start building stuff – and I don't mean on building sites, like the Boss did his whole life, earning zilch to come home dirty and worn out, his hands destroyed, and his back broken by the strain. I'd give anything to see some motivation on Foued's face when he decides to do some homework. But the pisser does bugger all.

Cat with Nine Lives

From now on, I'll think twice before using a phrase like 'hard as nails'. As of today, I know better than anybody just how hard nails really are – they may look tiny and trivial, but nails are the basis of everything. We don't pay nails enough attention, simple as.

The day before my stocktaking job, I got a phone call from the delightful Johanna at Temp Plus. It's already a result if you can understand what she's saying when you've got her in front of you, but on the telephone we're talking a miracle. It's like you want to give her some speech-therapy sessions for her birthday.

So she called me up to give me the instructions for my stocktaking 'assignment'.

'To be willing and motivated, to demonstrate to the person in charge that you deserve this opportunity, to wear the temping agency's badge with pride.'

They don't send just anybody to their clients. Especially when it involves spending a whole evening counting nails in an empty shop.

*   *   *

I got to Leroy Merlin with plenty of time to spare – I always like to be on the safe side. Punctuality's a disease with me. I can't stand people who are late, particularly the ones who don't think it matters. If someone makes me wait for long, I clear off, end of story. The Boss always says: 'If you wait for somebody once, you'll wait for them all your life.'

On site, I had to report to this woman called Sonia, who was a skinny dried-up thirty-something.

When all the team members had finally made it to the meeting point, she laid down the ground rules for our crazy evening ahead: a loo break *or* a cigarette break of no longer than ten minutes, so it was impossible to smoke *and* piss, you had to choose, unless you were up for doing both at the same time. Next, a strict ban on leaving the shop with your bag or jacket during the stocktake. What were they scared of? Someone jacking a washbasin on the sly?

Quick overview, most people were in their twenties, the majority were students and the group was mainly made up of boys.

Sonia divided us into pairs, one per aisle.

So I luck out and get the tools aisle with this short guy called Raphaël Vignon who doesn't say a word all evening. Great. There I am, stuck in this wack festival of nails, screws and bolts, with a guy who suffers from verbal constipation. I could tell he was giving me weird looks from time to time, so I carried on counting my nails like it was no big deal, but basically he gave me the creeps – empty shops are like underground car parks, they're the perfect scene for a murder. At certain points during the evening I'd almost manage to block him out, but then he'd start whistling, or coughing or whatever.

What a life. I could have landed any other team member, like the tall olive-skinned guy at the back, for example, who looked cute and fit, plus I'd noticed him sending a few interested glances my way. But no, I get locked with this Vignon guy, who looks like he goes around bumping off people's pets. It's just more of the same, I don't know why I'm still surprised I end up in these situations. It's my fate, so I should start getting used to it.

To top it all, my legs and back are killing me now. I've got these ugly marks on both knees, from being stuck up a stepladder for so long, and all for the grand sum of sixty-five euros. With a fortune like that, I can make two whole trips to the market.

I reckon I've done all the stupidest, most petty jobs you could imagine. Except maybe Father Christmas, outside the Galeries Lafayette.

I've been an activity leader for little kids on holiday camps. Peed pants, undone shoelaces, bogeys, tears and tantrums, I've been there. Paid peanuts, of course.

I've given out heart-shaped balloons on Valentine's Day at the shopping centre in Thiais. Seeing the most loved-up couples in Val-de-Marne kind of scarred me, because I got dumped the day before.

Next up came a wave of jobs in catering: McDonald's, Quick, Boulangerie Paul, KFC. I must have put on at least five kilos, but I lost them again when I was a waitress at *La Foire*, the bar that drives you crazy.

I even worked on a chatline. It paid well, and I went by the charming name of Samantha. But I soon cracked because it was too depressing. I quit on the evening this guy, who was a regular caller, begged me to do a chicken impression.

I've also done door-to-door sales for phone packages. I lost count of the number of times people slammed the door in my face, shouting: 'I don't believe in God, I'm not interested!'

Before that, I worked in telesales, flogging surveillance cameras. We took our numbers mainly from the 16th, 8th and 7th arrondissements. Every morning, this guy they called Cocaine would come and brief us in the office. He was trying to upload the software directly into our brains: 'Everyone's a winner, it's believing that matters! Today's going to be a great day!' Of course, he never forgot to slip in that the person who sold the most would get a bonus worth half their salary. I was kicked out after a week because I hadn't sold a single contract. It was too hard, I felt like I was working for the Home Office. And I'm not kidding, our job made things a lot easier for the police. Anyway, it was the only time in my life I've been over the moon to get the sack.

My last job was filling in for someone at Pizza Hut. Those words still go round in my head like some Machiavellian mantra: 'Thank you for choosing Pizza Hut, we hope to see you again soon, have a nice day.'

It's not like I don't aspire to something better, but you've got to live too. People who can fill their fridge doing something they love are so lucky. If that was me, I'd give thanks to God a lot more than five times a day, He'd deserve at least that.

Sometimes, I write things down in the spiral jotter I jacked from Leclerc. I write about what's happening in my life, what puts me in a good mood and what makes me pop a fuse. I keep telling myself that if I go crazy one of these days, like my dad, at least my story will be written down somewhere, and my children will be able to read about my dreams from these endz. I'm a bit of a cat, I feel like I've already led several lives. I'm twenty-four, going on forty.

You Need Two Hands to Clap

It's late and I've just got back. I bet they're sleeping like big babies, I could hear the Boss snoring from the entrance to our block. So here I am doing one of my least favourite things: opening our front door without making any noise, which is no mean feat, given the keys we've got – *sans soucis*, it's stamped on them, *no worries*. They're ENORMOUS, thirty centimetres long, eight wide, and they weigh in at fourteen kilos, they're like dungeon keys from the Roman Empire. Obviously I'm exaggerating, but you get the picture. Next up, I have to get undressed in the dark so as not to wake anybody, before sliding under my cold duvet. If I can get to sleep straight away, I'm in luck.

F.Y.I., I've just narrowly escaped being ambushed, Linda and Nawel, my wonderful unpredictable girlfriends, suggested a trip to the cinema. I knew their boyfriends would be tagging along too, but I had no idea they also had a Plan B – involving a blind date. As in, a friend of a friend of a friend. So, the guy in question, Hakim, is meant to be my knight in shining armour for the evening. I thought there was something up as soon as I saw the girls arrive. I can usually spot this kind of nightmare a mile off, so I should have realised what they were fixing up behind my back: *Gooseberry Gets Some Action of her Own*. When this guy in a baseball cap got out of his car and joined us, I clicked and nearly turned back, because I don't like surprises. But then I saw him front-on and there were one or two things in his favour, so I stayed. Trouble with eye candy is there's never anyone at home.

I got to choose the film – to the horror of the rest of the group, I picked this two-hour-long Belgian art-house feature (which turned out to be excellent, by the way). I had to listen to such brain-dead commentary from Dick-Head Hakim all the way through the film, I was ready to suffocate him. I could see the only people interested in the film were me and the two old ladies at the back (if you're good at maths, you'll have worked out there were eight of us in the cinema), but at least the others were keeping busy. They were playing at 'oral exploration', an activity that develops your sense of taste, touch, hearing and possibly even smell, all at the same time.

The weird thing is, everyone was starving when we came out of the cinema, so we went to grab something to eat, and this time, would you believe it, I didn't get to choose. Mouss, Nawel's boyfriend, has great taste, and he had the smart idea of taking us to a hip restaurant near Montparnasse, with seventies decor: the Space Shuttle. Perfect, except Dick-

Head Hakim's manners stuck out like a sore thumb in a trendy venue like that, just one word springs to mind, and that word is: 'bummer'.

The highlight of the evening was when we gave our order. Of course, Hakim decided to take charge. He called the waiter over, a tall blond skinny guy, kind of distinguished-looking, who stood bolt upright the way he'd been taught at catering college.

'Yo! Yo! Over here, innit, blud! You taking our order, cuz?'

You'd think we were at the fish stall in the covered market. In any other situation, it'd be LOL, but all I wanted to do was hide. In fact, if someone had suggested the burka right then, I'd have been so up for it. I ate my food like I was in mourning, and then made out I had a 'surprise migraine' so they had to drop me off at home. I ended up going round to Auntie Mariatou's for coffee, and telling her how mad the evening had turned out, but instead of being sympathetic she kept clucking like a turkey. Then she topped it all off with one of her magic sayings which can unravel difficult situations and relax tense atmospheres.

'Men are jackals, but show me the woman who can do without them? You need two hands to clap . . .'

Auntie's husband, Papa Demba, still looks at her with eyes full of admiration and love. He's adorable, solid and gentle, your ideal husband. And from what he's told me, their story is kind of extraordinary. Out of all the girls in the village, she was the one he noticed. One morning, when he was riding along in his cart, he saw her walking across a field. The picture of her that day has never left him – I reckon that's a subtle reference to her unforgettable backside – and from that moment on, he vowed she would be his betrothed. He belonged to a caste of blacksmiths and she came from a caste of nobles, so theirs was an impossible union, but Papa Demba's strength and determination won out against all odds.

I wet myself laughing when Auntie tells me stories about their relationship. She always says it's the woman who's responsible for the success of a couple and the man for its failure. Maybe that's pushing it a bit far, but that's Auntie Mariatou for you. She also says that love is like hair, you've got to keep it in tip-top condition.

I've confided in her ever since I was thirteen or fourteen. She gives spot-on advice. She's comforted me in times of heartache, she's encouraged me to be more confident in myself and she's even nudged me towards being more feminine, which was no small undertaking seeing as I used to be a real tomboy. Auntie hates all my baggy sweatshirts, low-slung jeans and trackie bottoms, so when I'm stupid enough to wear a baseball cap, it makes her spit. She introduced me to girlie clothes shops, high heels and make-up. It took me a while to get with the programme.

When I was sixteen or seventeen, and boys started showing an interest – because I finally looked a bit more like a girl and a bit less like a thug – I just thought they were taking the piss. That was when

Auntie reassured me, she used to say: 'You're pretty *and* clever, so let the boys drool. Take a look at the other girls and you'll soon see what you're worth. You know what they say: *Staring at empty plates makes you appreciate your dinner.*'

I must have been ten or eleven when I lost Mum and left Algeria for good with Foued in my arms. Over there, it was the other way round, I never saw any men. I just clung to my mum's skirts, and the skirts of the other women in the village too, because they were all responsible for educating the children and they stuck together. Sometimes, I would get slapped fifteen times for the same mistake. I lived among all these women who spent their lives hiding from men. I'd spend days at a time sorting out beads and ribbons for Mum, who was the village seam-stress. I stayed locked up in our hut. Luckily there was school, where I could talk to the other children, plus the little garden at the back of the house. I'd spend my free time at the foot of the orange tree, watching the street through the wire fencing and making up stories about the passers-by. One of the games I liked to play was recognising the fat ladies in their djellabas, the ones I'd seen at the hammam the day before. I even spotted the unlucky woman who'd rubbed my back with that horrible horsehair glove that left my skin raw, so I took a sneaky pleasure in chucking a few stones her way.

When we turned up at Ivry, to live with the Boss, so much freedom and fresh air came as a shock. He let me play by myself outside, and he often took me to the PMU bar. While he was filling out his horse-racing tickets, triple forecast, I remember he'd give me enough change for a few goes on the slot machine. Afterwards, if I'd won, I was allowed a big cup of hot chocolate. And even if I lost, I still got one. That's why no one can beat me today. On the estate, I used to play football with all the boys, and I'd pull the girls' hair and jack their skipping rope to whip them with, just like the boys did. I went straight from an all-female environment to a world of men, with no stopover.

When I hit my teens it got complicated, because I was an early developer.

I was so ashamed of my boobs that I hid them under these gigantic jumpers that were ten times too big for me, and to make matters worse I was the only girl in the class who was fully equipped. The other girls, who were still kind of flat all over, were jealous of me. If only they knew how much I was squashing my so-called assets so they didn't look as big . . .

My first real trauma happened the first time I had my period. I got it into my head that I wasn't long for this world. I remember writing these farewell letters, fearing the worst, the kind of stuff you only imagine in the twilight of your life, like 'fessing up to Elie Allouche I had a crush on him. All the girls at school reckoned Smelly Elie, as he was known, was a plonker, but I thought he was kind of cute. I was so convinced my bleeding was a sign of my imminent death, that I nearly made the fatal mistake of giving all my Boyz II Men tapes to Bouchra, the class neek who I used to bully and pick on to make her do my homework for me. I was losing it.

Luckily, Auntie Mariatou was there to guide me at times like that; she went out of her way to help me and my brother and tried to make up for our mum not being around.

Now, I know when you turn fourteen or fifteen, everyone calls it a 'challenging phase' – and that's why I'm doing my best to be behind Foued all the way. I remember what a walking disaster I was, back in the day. I was always outside, fighting tooth and nail. When the neighbours told Dad about it, he'd give me such a blasting, telling me to go and wash my mouth out, with a big fat block of Marseille soap, but nothing doing, a week later I'd start all over again.

I was tough, plus I fought like a man. I didn't scratch and I didn't slap but if I had beef with some-body I'd use my fists, my feet, my knees, and sometimes I'd even go for a headbutt too.

In Algeria, the first part of my education was in a small community school where girls and boys weren't allowed to sit next to each other. We had this deep respect for school and we always treated a teacher with deference. So in class, when the teacher asked a student a question, you had to stand to answer. And if one of us got caught cheating or talking, we'd be punished straight away with a cruel metal ruler; the noise was so horrible that everybody shared in the pain.

My mum and my aunts would often remark that a teacher was like a second father and it was right and proper for him to punish me; they even pointed out that they should punish me a second time, to back him up. A second father sounded like a weird idea to me. I hardly knew the first. He was this man who lived in France to work and send us back money, so we could eat properly and have nice dresses to wear for Eid-el-Kebir. I saw him for two weeks a year during the holidays. He didn't say much, but he was always giving me hundred dinar notes so I could buy nice things. I kept pestering him with questions. I'd ask him what it was like to go up into the sky, and how come the aeroplane stayed up there? He never gave me a scientific explanation, it was always something far out, I do remember that . . .

When I arrived in this cold land of distrust, I was a polite and enthusiastic little girl, but I turned into real bitch in less time than you could say the word. I soon dropped my good old ways, like that business of standing to talk to the teacher for example. The first few times I did that over here, the other students just burst out laughing. I went bright red and they were all going: 'Teacher's suck-up!'

I quickly realised that I had to assert myself, so that's what I did. I've come a long way since then. As the powers-that-be would say, I've become a perfect example of integration.

Almost French. The only thing missing is the stupid bit of laminated sky-blue paper stamped with love and good taste, the famous *French touch*. That tiny scrap would give me my rights and release me from getting up at three o'clock in the morning every three months to go and join the queue in front of the immigration office, in the cold, to renew my stay for the umpteenth time.

Then again, sometimes you get to meet interesting people in those queues. Last time, I was having a conversation with this guy from Eastern Europe, I can't remember which country. Tonislav, he was called. He was offering me a deal on these Diesel jeans, half the price you'd pay in the shops. Hanging out together in the queue helped pass the time, plus the more I looked at him, the more cute I reckoned he was in his beat-up biker's jacket . . . But it'd just be plain stupid, if you're going to get involved with a guy, he might as well have his residency papers sorted. I'm fed up of being a foreigner.

There are two other blokes I often see, two Turks from Izmir, they're brothers. One day, when everybody was waiting in the pouring rain, one of them was really sweet and lent me his umbrella – I was so touched that he didn't mind getting wet for me. Ever since, when we run into each other, we get talking and they're always inviting me to eat at this kebab shop where they work. 'Free. No problems. Greek, kebabs.' I'll go one of these days, I can picture where it is, just opposite the station, it's called the Bodrum Sun, just like three-quarters of the kebab joints in France . . .

So I've met a few nice people, but it's not exactly a non-stop party atmosphere in front of the immigration office. Generally, the police treat us like we're animals. They talk to us like we're halfwits, those silly bitches behind that bloody glass screen that keeps them far from the reality of our lives, and more often than not they don't even bother looking us in the eye.

Last time, this old man who was Malian, I think, missed his turn because he didn't recognise his name. The woman called out Mr Wakeri, once, twice, three times before moving on to the next person without a thought. He'd been waiting there since dawn and his name was Mr Bakeri, that's why he didn't stand up. Someone spoke to him in Bambara, explaining that his name had definitely been called already; she tried to negotiate for him to take his turn at the booth, because he hardly spoke any French, but it was too late. They made him come back the following morning.

I remember one day I just lost it. I was exhausted. I'd finished working at the bar at one o'clock in the morning, and the customers had been extra shitty that shift. I could feel how close I was to the edge. By 4 a.m., I was already queuing in the cruel cold, but my number didn't come up until one o'clock. So I was in no mood for the way that old trollop in the booth was disrespecting me to my face. Luckily for her, I wasn't the impulsive fourteen-year-old I used to be, or she'd have been dead, drowned in her own saliva. I just shouted like a silly idiot, but it was pointless because as soon as she gave the signal the guys in uniform turned up to throw me out.

When things had cooled off a bit, I felt pretty stupid. The bottom line was, I hadn't even sorted my papers. I had to come back the next day, defeated, eyes lowered, and of course with my luck I landed the same employee as the day before. One thing was clear, she didn't remember me.

Since the decree of February 2006 and its aim of expelling 25,000 people a year, it's like there's a smell of gas in the queue in front of the immigration office. You hear worrying rumours about ambushes as if there's a war going on, including this grim story a woman told me while we were waiting by the booths. Her cousin had been summoned to the immigration office. He was very happy about it, because he'd been waiting for months. He thought he'd be able to legalise his situation at last, but it was a trap. They took him to a detention centre and now he's back in Bamako. He didn't even have time to say goodbye to his nearest and dearest or to pick up his belongings. Since I heard about that, whenever I'm sitting on those hard uncomfortable chairs at the immigration office, I'm imagining that the men with small moustaches in their offices only have to press a button for my chair to turn into an ejector seat and I'll find myself back in the village.

Rainbow After Weeks of Rain

Today, it's the Boss's birthday. To mark the occasion, I made some *kerentita*, using a recipe I got from my grandmother Mimouna – she taught me how to make it back in Algeria. It's this cake baked with chickpea flour, and it's a typical dish from the west of the country. I can still remember how, early in the morning, the street vendor would go round the block on his old bicycle shouting out: 'Here it is, come and get it, come and get your *kerentita*!' And then me and my cousins would come running out of our place, barefoot, and we'd only be wearing our *gandouras* but we didn't care. Uncle Khaled always threw a fit: 'Get back inside right now, you girls are crazy! Do you want to be seen like that? Men will look at you, the shame! Get back inside!'

It was a laugh, but if we took too long then it stopped being funny because Uncle Khaled would get out his legendary plastic sandal. I still haven't worked out what his technique was, but he never missed his target. It didn't matter where he threw that sandal from, it would spin one way and then the other, and always end up exactly where it was meant to. In your back, mostly. Respect, Uncle Khaled! After several years of practice, he was the African plastic-sandal-throwing champion.

'So, how old am I?'

'Sixty-one, Dad.'

'*Ooh la la*, no, no, we can't celebrate that!'

'Why not?'

'It's a feast for fools, a party for wrinklies clapping each other because they're one step closer to the grave . . .'

'No, you mustn't say that, it's a good excuse for all three of us to have a party.'

I gave him his best suit and his most handsome tie to wear. The Boss was happy, I could tell. Me and Foued had pulled out all the stops: cake, candles, even the song. So of course that witch of a neighbour goes and bangs on the ceiling with her broom. Does she really think that's going to stop me from singing? If she doesn't let up, I'll go down and break her body in two. Basically, we couldn't have cared less, we probably sang even louder just to get on her nerves, stupid old cow, and singing made all three of us happy. I enjoy these rainbow moments after weeks of rain.

After that, I shut myself in my room to listen to the Diam's CD I stole from Leclerc last week – come to think of it, gotta stop jacking gear, I'm past the age limit. I'm in front of my mirror with the deodorant for a mike and I'm singing, like a nutter. If you could see me now! Doesn't take much to cheer me up. I'm happy – it never lasts of course but it feels *nice* when it happens. I'm like a mad woman, I sing louder and louder, I turn up the volume on the stereo and jump as high as I can. The music's carrying me away now and I start dreaming about a Diam's concert: she invites me onstage to do a duo, we rap in front of a euphoric crowd, I'm loving it, I lift up my arms, my stomach's queasy, my heart's racing. She lets me step into the spotlight and gets the audience to chant my name, so everyone's shouting: 'AHLÈME! AHLÈME!' When it's all over, we exit via the stage wings, exhausted but totally elated. Diam's looks as slick as ever, her mascara hasn't run, she's not even sweating. As for me, three members of staff rush towards me with face sponges and make-up remover pads. Then we talk about 'how it was for us' as we sip a glass of Tropicana in the dressing rooms.

A series of knocks brings me back to reality. That ugly cow of a neighbour – stupid AND a government employee, I ask you – is banging again. I've got her all worked up with this rap concert business, but I don't give a shit. She can knock till her arm drops off, she can even call the police if she likes, I'll just ask them to dance with me. We'll do a remake: 'Dance with the Po-Po'.

The phone ringing completes my return to earth. It's that girl again who won't stop calling the house to speak to Foued. I always tell her he's sleeping, or having a shower or out, even if he's in his bedroom. She gets on my nerves, phoning all the time. I don't like the sound of her voice, and she's not impressing me either. I reckon she's a silly bitch who wears padded bras and loudmouths her mum. I don't trust her. Sometimes Foued'll ask me: 'Who was that on the phone?' So I gulp and lie: 'Someone from the council' or 'My friend Linda.' You should always gulp before lying, makes it easier to swallow.

I couldn't tell you why I do it. Maybe I shouldn't, but I can't stop myself. When it comes to my little brother, I try to act in his best interests. And when it comes to girls, there's no rush. He needs to concentrate on school for the time being. He can have a girlfriend over the summer, when he's far from home, like on summer camp. At least that way I won't need to know anything about it. Between now and then, he'll have installed a bit more software on his hard drive. So for the time being, that little bitch can just get on with her trashy magazine questionnaires and leave my brother in peace.

He's up against it at college right now. Only last week, I was called in by the education adviser, and it didn't go so well. Let's just say we didn't really connect. First of all, I'm not here to take lessons from anybody. Plus, I hated the attitude of that poor woman in her over-ironed blouse. She was full of all those good intentions and ready-made expressions you find in books, along the lines of: 'working in challenging environments', 'changing the world', and even 'finding yourself among the poor'. She read out some of the discipline reports from the teachers who've excluded Foued from their classes, and you could tell she was getting a kick out of it. 'Rude', 'violent', 'disrespectful' were the three most common adjectives. I was having a hard time believing they meant my little brother, but when I looked more closely at some of the reports, I recognised his tag and if I'm honest it was kind of funny.

Student Foued Galbi urinated in the wastepaper basket at the back of the classroom while I had my back turned, and a foul smell invaded my lesson. I will no longer tolerate this animal behaviour.

Mr Costa, Mathematics teacher

Foued G. is a troublemaker. He clowns about and deliberately plays for laughs instead of working. He waits until everybody's quietly getting on with their worksheets to put on a silly voice and pronounce vulgar or embarrassing words such as 'COCK' or 'PRICK' or 'JIMMIE'. The whole class bursts out laughing and I'm forced to do the police act again to calm them down.

Mrs Fidel, Spanish teacher

Report by Mr Denoyer, Combined Sciences teacher

Foued Galbi threatens me in the middle of class. I quote: 'I know where you live, you bastard!' 'I'm going to smash your face in, you dickhead, geddout!'

Moreover, yesterday, Wednesday 16th, hidden behind a column in the corridor, he blatantly insulted me, and I quote: 'Denoyer, your head is deformed', 'Denoyer, you lard arse', 'Denoyer, your wife is fat.'

Before that, on a day scheduled for a test, he had stuck chewing gum into the lock of the classroom door. I couldn't open up and the test had to be postponed. I demand sanctions that are appropriate to the seriousness of these acts and above all to the words of this young man, by which I mean no less than a disciplinary committee followed by expulsion.

I asked this education adviser, who was full of shit, if excluding a fifteen-year-old kid because he's pointed out that his teacher has a fat arse, might not be an overreaction. All she said was that, in any case, he wouldn't have to go to school in a few months' time and that, if he carried on down this road, expulsion would be the only course of action left open to them.

I ended our meeting by saying exactly what she'd been hoping to hear: I'd get him to pull his socks up, it wouldn't happen again, give him a week and he would even be an algebra whizz. Spit and shake on it.

These teachers, I'm telling you . . . I had the same kinds of bullshitters, who only do the job because the holidays suit them, oh and their favourite moment in the day is the holy coffee break.

I finally got out of that awful office with its prevention posters and pet photos all over the walls. Half an hour in there told me all I needed to know about that woman. She's basically very lonely, watching all the illusions she ever had about her job come crashing down around her. So she tries putting up a front, and it shows. She wants to convince herself she's doing useful work here. She was still a believer right up until a few days ago, when the corpse of Ambrose, the college goldfish she used to feed so lovingly, was found dead at the bottom of Mrs Rozet's locker – that slag of a PE teacher. With a bit of luck the poor adviser will get a transfer from these endz, and it'll be better for everybody.

When You're in Love, Who's Counting?

The men in green uniforms are closing in on me.

'You're sick in the head! We told you to use one! Now you're really in the shit –'

'Yeah, yeah, all right, you don't need to bang on about it, I know. I'll just have to live with my mistake, that's all! I forgot, it was an accident, I didn't stop to think.'

'D'you realise how crazy this is? I mean, talk about stupid, you had one on you. All you had to do was use it! And it's not like you can afford to make a mistake like that. What are you going to do?'

'Yeah, OK, thanks, it's done now, so stop mouthing off at me, it's not like it's going to change anything. I'll get myself out of this mess, it's fine . . .'

The girls are right, what was I thinking? I'm screwed, it's not like I can undo my mistake now, I'll have to pay the price for not thinking first.

'Tickets!'

I show him my identity card straight up, so he can slap on the fine. No point arguing, I can already see from his depressed seagull's face that there's no way out.

Linda and Nawel, model citizens and suck-ups of the system, show their Navigo passes like sensible girls. They take their tickets back with their goody-two-shoes, law-abiding smiles.

I give in and hand over my magnificent green passport justifying my existence. The inspector's sick-bird eyes come to rest on the exotic words inscribed on it: 'The People's Democratic Republic of Algeria'. I can see he's in a tight spot here, his head's spinning, he's coming unhinged, he needs his meds and fast.

'You don't have any documentation in French?'

'Why don't you start by opening it? You'll see it's bilingual, it's got your language inside too.'

'Don't get cheeky with me, young lady, or things could turn ugly, I'm reminding you that you are in contravention of the law.'

All this because I didn't jam that stupid bit of purple card into their blimmin' machine . . .

So I shut it, seeing as here like everywhere, when you're on the wrong side of the law, you shut it. I've got no desire to spend my afternoon down the station, because the Feds, well, that's a whole other story . . .

The RATP inspectors clear off, satisfied they're doing their job properly, leaving me with a slip of blue paper that sentences me to pay sixty-two euros. So I'm forced to inject an outrageous sum of money into our drug-addicted state that just keeps coming back for more. The girls offer to help me pay. I turn them down, it wouldn't be right, plus it's not exactly like they're insisting. Then they start going on about their Valentine's evening, the candlelit dinner, what present they got and other stuff you don't normally talk about on buses, at this hour, on a market day.

At first, I listen and join in. But when the topic turns to love, I zone out. While the wifeys are swapping stories about their Valentine's treats, I notice a young couple on my right. They're well dressed and they smell of perfume. The guy's used a squirt of gel on his hair, and the girl a trace of eyeliner on her eyes. They're so into each other, it's hard to describe. I can't get over how in love they are, they stare into each other's eyes, all the way to the back of the retina, and I bet they could keep it up for hours. They touch each other discreetly, they smile at each other. Then he starts kissing her on the neck and the girl quivers like a chicken, you can tell it makes her feel good. After that, the guy dives deep into her throat, like an orphaned baboon. You'd think you were watching a wildlife documentary.

I was in love too once, but not in public, not like that – at least, I don't think so, or maybe I don't remember properly. It was so long ago . . .

Couples, I keep seeing them everywhere at the moment. They mainly come out when the weather starts getting better. They go to the parks, the cafés, the cinemas and they flaunt it in public, everywhere's heaving with people in love. They act like nothing else exists around them.

When you feel like that, you've got such a tiny fraction of common sense left, anything goes. As a rule of thumb, I'd say you lose at least half your intellectual capacity, maybe more.

And if you're foolish in love, then you're *really* stupid in heartbreak . . . You spend your time blubbing, you blub till you trash your last remaining scrap of Kleenex, and then you start losing weight, you burn up an unbelievable number of calories.

It's crazy how sadness is the best diet, ten times more effective than all those miracle step-plans, 'How to lose weight in time for summer', that clutter the magazines.

At times like this, your friends get really worried and keep asking you if you're feeling any *better* – not just if you're fine, like before.

You increase your coffee intake, ditto cigarettes, alcohol and maybe drugs . . . You start listening to sad songs, and watching tear-jerkers on telly. You need to talk a lot and end up with ten-page phone bills. It really is the only thing you can think about. You've had warnings at work, you're close to being fired, and it's weird but you're sort of thinking *bring it on*. At home, you start breaking plates and stuff, you accidentally trash the best dinner service, a family heirloom. You can hardly bear to look at your face in the mirror: it's so swollen and puffed up with tears, you don't think it's ever been this ugly. And when you finally try to make an effort, you can't even put your lipstick on without bursting into tears. At one point, you manage to 'fess up to that loudmouth neighbour that you couldn't care less about her sick uncle in Brittany, or her pussy's hot flushes that come on so dramatically not even the vet can do anything about them.

You're like, who gives a fuck about that or anything else?

And then one morning you realise something's changed, it's not such a heavy load any more, you feel better, you can sleep at night, you head out each day and you have the strength to carry on.

Not long after, you bump into the person in question in the street. And it just so happens on that particular day you're looking hideously ugly, we're talking the kind of ugliness you only go in for once a year. Bam, that's when you bump into him.

It always happens that way. Nothing like the moment you'd imagined inside out and back to front, the film of your reunion that you've screened inside your head hundreds of times, rewinding and playing again so as not to miss out a single detail. But no screenplay could touch this catastrophic reality. You're dressed like a tramp, the bags under your eyes are sagging down to the bottom of your cheeks, and you're sporting a haircut straight out of an eighties soap opera. That's just the way it is, a formula as tried and tested as 'the car next to ours is faster' or 'the food on my neighbour's plate looks tastier'. You've got no choice but to jet, dodge him at all costs while sending up a frantic prayer he hasn't seen anything.

I vaccinated myself against ever going there again. I promised myself that in future I would beware of nice men, the ones who hold the door open for you, pay the bill, turn up to dates on time and actually listen to what you're saying; because they've got to be hiding something. I'll avoid that kind of a guy like the plague. He's the one who leaves you an emotional wreck, heart and Kleenex all wrung out.

He tells you he loves you, and then shows you the photo of his wife and kids, pride of place in his wallet, bang in the middle of all his credit cards.

He tells you you're the woman of his dreams, and then all of a sudden he leaves you because you're too good for him. You've got no idea what's going on until the day when you see him strolling around, relaxed as you like, with his ex – so basically you're the ex, now.

He thinks you're beautiful, clever, gentle and witty, and he's always borrowing money off you – but when you're in love, who's counting? Until one morning you call him to tell him you love him, like you do every morning, but surprise surprise, what you get is the cold, cynical female voice of his mobile-phone provider. She informs you that the number you've dialled doesn't exist any more, you won't be hearing from him again.

Or else he comes to pick you up in his metallic-grey Ford Focus, opens the car door for you, asks if you've had a good day, and compliments you on your outfit. As for you, you're feeling pretty, you keep giving him these loving glances and telling yourself he's the one for you. When the two of you get out of the wib, he rearranges his nuts and then burps. You think it's kind of disgusting but you fancy him anyway. Next, he makes a show of using the remote central locking, *tut-tut*, over his shoulder. Well classy, you think, he's got style, you like it, you love him. He tells you he's taking you out to a restaurant – makes a nice change. Seeing as you're a secret fan of Sunday-afternoon weepies on the telly, you think he's going to pop the question. But in the middle of your I'm-on-a-diet salad, he explains he's met someone else, she's great, this girl, and he's moving to Grenoble with her. He'll be packing up next week, so he'd appreciate it if you could give him back that drill he lent you along with his Barry White CDs. Oh and by the way, shall we go Dutch?

I've cried a lot over men. And then regretted it afterwards, telling myself they're all bastards – all girls say that – and none of them deserves my tears. Then again, it doesn't take much to make me blub. I'll burst into tears in front of the most stupid television programmes: the child reunited with his mother or the unemployed bloke who gets a job, I melt every time.

On the day Auntie Mariatou gave birth, I wasn't just the only white in the clinic waiting room, I was also the only one to cry too. The others were giving me these sidelong glances and wondering if I was there for the same reason as them. It's as if I'm making up for all those years when my eyes didn't have any tears.

I didn't cry when Mum died. To be honest, I don't think I understood what was going on.

It was the wedding day of fat Djamila, a distant cousin who lived in a neighbouring village. Mum had undertaken to sew all the clothes in Djamila's trousseau. I can still see myself crouching down close to her, watching. She fascinated me, I could spend hours like that watching her at work. With her slender, delicate fingers she would embroider the Algiers jacket with golden thread, following the curves of the design accurately and carefully, without ever going over the line or needing to start again. For months on end, she worked on completing seven traditional outfits for the bride. It wasn't a small job: a huge amount of material and beads were needed, because the bride in question weighed a hundred kilos.

I remember those long afternoons when the women from the village would talk about nothing but the big event. Zineb and Samira, the cooks, were always jabbering away and laughing about Djamila behind her back.

'You'll see, when it comes to the wedding, it'll rain all day long. You know what they say: it's bad luck for a young girl to take the lid off the kitchen pot behind her mother's back, to have a taste before meal-time, it means there'll be rain on her wedding day. Well, she's fatter than Belbachir's cows so she must have sneaked that lid off an awful lot of times!'

'You're not wrong there, I wonder if she'll be able to fit into the dresses Sakina's killing herself to sew for her . . .'

And then they chuckled like hens. I thought they were right bitches and wondered how they dared be so rude about Djamila behind her back, opening their poisonous mouths to flash a few rotten teeth, without feeling any guilt. Mum balled them out, she said they were just two jealous and bitter old gossips and that God would punish them for saying things like that. She was shouting in the middle of the courtyard: 'One morning, you'll wake up without your tongues, inshallah.'

I'd have done anything to go to the party, I was so desperate to be there. I was only eleven and I begged Mum to take me with her. But she refused, point-blank. I even offered to sort out her big pile of ribbons and offcuts for her, to clean the stable, milk the cow every morning, go round to Aïsha the witch to pick up the wool; but nothing doing, I had to look after my little brother who was just a baby, plus she wouldn't be able to keep an eye on me, she'd be too busy dressing the bride. She was also worried about the long journey to reach the village. 'These days, the roads aren't safe any more, the whole country is infested with trick roadblocks, I don't want anything to happen to you.'

And what about her, wouldn't anything happen to her? I could feel how tense things were at the time. We weren't allowed to listen to music too loudly any more, I remember, especially love songs, and certain words could no longer be said outside the home. People were constantly frightened, curtains had been taken down from the windows to make way for bars. Uncle Khaled didn't want us to put a foot outside the house now, not even to buy our slices of *kerentita* – in any case, the street vendor no longer came round our way.

It was the day of the wedding and death struck savagely. It came in a team, set its sights on this tiny village where, if only for an evening, joy had reigned. It was a massacre, no other word for it, no more women ululating, just the sound of wailing. They killed everybody, even the children, babies as tiny as Foued. And it wasn't the only village to be razed to the ground. So people didn't celebrate weddings much after that, they were traumatised by those images of mutilated bodies and babies' bottles stained with blood. I remember having this dream where the dresses my darling mother had sewn so carefully were bloodstained. It was Mum who chose to call me Ahlème. My name means 'dream' in Arabic. And my mum's dream was that one day she'd see me parading in the seven traditional outfits of the bride, when my turn came. I haven't set foot in Algeria since, I don't know if that's out of fear or something else. I hope I'll have the strength to go back there one day, to feel the earth of my *bled* again, the warmth of the people, and to forget the smell of blood.

No Such Thing as Random

The Boss is having an afternoon nap, I'm dreaming about a better life and there are students demonstrating in the streets of Paris. The local police station just called the flat to tell us we need to go and pick up Foued. My little brother round at the pigs? It was a big shock. If I'd got a penalty fare from the RATP at that age, the Boss would have had an epileptic fit and given me a blasting to remember; he taught us to respect authority, or he tried at any rate.

It always amazes me, this funny gratitude the Boss and the other men of his age feel towards their host country. You walk in the shadows, you pay your rent on time, clean police record, not five minutes of unemployment in forty years of jobbing it, and after that, you take off your hat, you smile and say: '*Merci la France!*'

I've often wondered how a man like the Boss, who considers pride to be a vital organ, was able to keep his head down all those years before totally losing it. I'm not going to wake him up to tell him that his only son is round the Feds, there's no point, let him be. I watch him sleeping and he looks old and tired. My poor Boss seems worn out, knackered from making the pneumatic drill, his old dance partner, waltz with no let-up, knackered from having led a tumultuous tango with 'Franzza' for nearly forty years. Not that it leaves any bitter aftertaste in his mouth, just the chaos in his head . . .

Why does Foued have to make my life so difficult? Just recently, he promised me he'd calm down, make an effort at school; he knows he can't afford to mess up, I thought he'd understood but, like Auntie Mariatou says, 'When the snake is still, that doesn't mean it's a branch.'

And now the little shit's making me set foot round at the uniforms, and I'm fuming.

Right there, at the entrance to the pig pen, I see a familiar face from the immigration office. It's Tonislav, the buff guy in his old leather jacket. I see him pushing his way through, frowning. I grab his arm as he passes by and he's startled, he jumps.

'Hey, gorgeous, you gave me a scare! How's it going?'

'Good, thanks. What about you, Tonislav, every-thing fine?'

'I'm always OK! So what are you doing here?'

'I've got to pick up my little brother, he must have done something stupid.'

'Ouch! Well, don't be too tough on him . . .'

'Yeah, yeah, we'll see about that . . . Anyway, nice to bump into you – how random is that?'

'Random? Let me tell you something, there's no such thing as random, that's just for fools.'

'For fools, is that right?'

'Yeah, but how about meeting up when it's not so random . . . ?'

He raises an eyebrow and looks straight at me. I laugh, and so does he. His big blue eyes crinkle and two cute little dimples show up on his cheeks, and for the first time I notice he's got this silver tooth flaunting it over the others. The guy's got me hot and bothered. He's handsome, no denying it. I give him my phone number and he slips it proudly into the pocket of his beaten-up leather jacket. He's right, I'd like to see him again, and I don't mean in a random way.

I'm talking to this fat perverted Fed, who's staring at my boobs like they're my eyes. He reminds me of Francky Vincent, with his thin moustache and lechy looks. He asks me to hold on and points to a coffee machine, a sure sign I'm going to have to wait longer than five minutes. I could have done with a shot of the black stuff, but the machine's out of order – that would have been asking too much. I pace up and down, my heels make this nasty clacking noise against the tiled floor. It echoes everywhere, it does my head in. In the end I sit down again. I think about Tonislav and start dreaming about love, in the middle of the reception area at the police station.

Loads of people file past in front of me. This woman comes to lodge a complaint against her boss. At the top of her voice, she's saying how it's sexual harassment because he can't keep his hands off her arse and orders her about: 'Get me a coffee, bitch! Photocopy that for me, bitch!' That's when I realise there's a lack of fucking privacy in police stations. Even if you're just waiting for some kind of documentation, you get to hear everybody's stories.

Suddenly, I spot my brother's friends, the Villovitch brothers, handcuffed to a bunch of smug pigs, and that's when I click that it's a family affair. My brother's been taken in for questioning about a scam that stinks, which he's more than capable of organising if I know my brother, because Foued's problem is he's a leader not a follower.

Francky gives me these drooling looks from time to time. I'll have been waiting for an hour soon. I decide to ask him again exactly when I might be able to collect my little brother, and that's when the bugger swears he'd clean forgotten why I came. No shit. So I follow his directions and make my way over to a door without even bothering to guess whether his hungry eyes are following my *zerk*. I try to keep my cool and God knows it's not easy. There, in a small office that's too brightly lit, Foued is sitting on a bench. He doesn't dare look me in the eye when he sees me come into the room, he lowers his gaze instead. He's ashamed, and so he should be. My brother is handcuffed to the radiator on the wall, and it hurts me in a way the boys in blue can't begin to imagine. Starsky and Hutch make me step outside the office so they can explain the story to me: a big stand-off between the kids on Uprising Estate, including Foued and his friends, and the ones from the neighbouring Yuri Gagarin Estate. According to the Feds, the kids had been dabbling in fraud. My little brother and his mates had resold a stash of DVDs for one of the older guys from the estate opposite, but they didn't give him his money because he didn't want to pay them enough, so basically it's your average mess-up, just a bunch of stupid kids who haven't got a clue. Plus, Navarro and the gang found a tear-gas cannister, a window-smasher and a butcher's knife in Foued's bomber jacket. I'd been wondering about that knife, I'd turned the whole kitchen over looking for it.

That said, the butt-useless brigade was right, it could have turned very nasty. One of the kids is in hospital; as for my brother, his teeth are smashed in and his mouth's puffed up big time. You'd think he'd had a collagen injection or something.

I don't mouth off at the little shit. And believe me, I want to: there's nothing I'd like better than to wring him out limb from limb. But I'm not reacting. I'm past it. I'm stuck at this version of little Foufou drinking hot chocolate with me, the two of us watching cartoons on TV together before school, so I don't even have the strength to hit the bastard where it hurts.

I hope the Boss'll still be asleep when we get back.

Hot Date

I've fixed myself up for our date. I spent two hours in the bathroom. I applied mascara to make my lashes look longer, a padded bra for extra boob definition, I straightened my hair, put on a moisturising face mask and offered up a prayer for my salvation. I thought about wearing a skirt, but I never know what to do in those things. I'd have to remember to keep my legs together the whole time I was sitting down, and tug at it if it climbed too high when I was walking. In the end I go for jeans, otherwise there's just too much to keep on top of . . .

Of course, I don't forget the final touch, squirting myself all over with perfume. Aim of the day: to remind him of the sweets from his childhood. I pull out all the stops, I even wear high heels. I've got butterflies, I'm flustered, I bump into things and then at one point I stop and ask myself why am I putting myself through all this?

On the phone, he said to meet at five o'clock at a café in the Place d'Italie and then he let it drop that he'd be there from quarter to. So I'm aiming for twenty to.

The café's called the Balto, like most cafés. Maybe, later on, this place will become 'our' café. Maybe, in a few years' time, we'll remember this day, and get all choked up as we talk about it. Yeah, so I'm getting carried away – and? Don't I have the right to, for once?

I sit down and order a *café serré*. Next to me, a fat woman with her hair pulled back in a big bun is counting out the number of two-centime pieces spread over the table. 'Eighty-eight, ninety, ninety-two, ninety-four, ninety-eight, one hundred and two . . . er . . . oh shit! Bugger! Two, four, six, eight . . .' I scald my lips on the boiling coffee while the barman dries his glasses methodically. He's whistling a tune I don't recognise but then he starts singing a Jacques Brel number, and that's when it gets complicated. I can tell the fat woman with the bun is about to lose it and then, all of a sudden, she deliberately scatters all the coins she'd so carefully laid out in little piles in front of her.

'Shit, Diego! Sing in your head, I can't concentrate!'

'It's my bar, isn't it? I'll sing if I want to.'

'You're getting on my nerves, I'm trying to count.'

'You've just got to lay off the booze, Rita, then you'll be able to count more quickly!'

At which point the fat hysterical woman turns sharply to me.

'What about you, young lady? Can you count quickly?'

Without giving me any time to answer, she grabs

fistfuls of her coins and sends them flying all over my table. She chucks them everywhere, there's even one that lands in my cup. Rita plunges two of her fat stubby fingers into my coffee to recover a portion of her fortune. So, I carry out Big Bun's orders. I sift the change conscientiously and do the maths: there are exactly four euros and thirty-eight centimes. Satisfied, she tidies the nest egg into a Monoprix bag, leaving eight centimes on my table: 'Keep them, darling, you deserve it!'

At which point Tonislav pushes open the door of the Balto. It's like a scene straight out of a film, he enters in a beam of light, I see everything in slow motion, I can even hear the music playing inside my head. It's all set for a jaw-dropping entrance. Tousled hair, three-day stubble, holes in his jeans and he's wearing that battered leather biker jacket he never takes off. But I still think he looks fit, so it was worth me spending weeks in the bathroom. I'm feeling awkward and shallow now . . .

It all happens so fast after that, he gives me his *Dead Poets' Society* smile, comes over and kisses me like it's the most natural thing in the world, like it's something he does every day, as ordinary as tying his laces or lighting a cigarette. He blows me away, this guy, he's got me transfixed. Then he sits down next to me, laid-back as you like.

So I'm sitting there, eyes popping out of my head, when Big Bun gives this hoot of laughter that makes me look even more of a fool.

This is too much, I'm feeling feverish. Then I notice

that Tonislav's laughing and I join in, which eases the tension.

When I tell the girls about it, they'll never believe me, but I swear on my mum's grave I'm telling the truth: normally, I'd never let someone kiss me on the first date! But this time – knock me down with a branch from the baobab tree – the guy shows up, goes straight for my mouth, like it's no big deal at all . . . without me signing anything beforehand, no email alert, as in I really wasn't ready, you get me.

Then we talk for hours, and I drink up his words like I'm a beginner. He tells me loads of far out stories, and I believe in him like you believe in Father Christmas when you're four. He tells me about his life in Belgrade, how he used to organise wild dogfights for a living when he was a skint teenager, or later on how he taught the violin in an all-girls' school. They must have been slobbering over him like snails. If I'd had a teacher who looked like Tonislav, I'd never have left school at sixteen.

Actually, he's a serious musician, he's been playing the violin for years, he taught himself on his dad's violin, or so he says. He used to steal scores from the national conservatoire and then he'd just figure it out.

What worries me, big time, is that even though I hardly know this guy, I totally lose it when I'm with him, it's like there's no map, all I can do is laugh like an idiot at everything he says. *Wesh?* Wassup? This isn't me, this silly bitch wearing loads of make-up, clucking round him like a farmyard hen.

The Boss Loses Face

Today my father is no longer a man. It's all falling apart.

The Boss wanted to trim his magnificent moustache, but he miscalculated, his mind must have been somewhere else, and he missed. When I got home, I found that fool Foued pissing himself laughing. As for the poor Boss, he was in bed, lying on his back with a chunk of moustache in his hand. There was just a shapeless reminder above his lips. I felt so sorry for him, stretched out like that, like an aged cancer patient on his deathbed.

'What happened, Dad?'

'I've been given the Eye! Someone cast the *aïn* on me!'

'No they haven't, no one's given you the Eye, you just didn't shave properly, that's all!'

'So why's *he* laughing like that?'

We could hear the high-pitched sniggering of the little shit coming from the living room.

'Foued! Shut it! Dad, come on, I'll shave it all off, and that way it'll grow back good and proper.'

'I'm not a man any more! My son has more of a moustache than me! I don't go out any more, I don't go to work any more.'

'It's all right, moustaches grow back.'

'I've lost my honour! I earned that honour. I used to carry the flag high! I was proud and I looked up to the sky!'

And he starts singing the Algerian national anthem as he stares at the ceiling. Then he signals to me to come over.

'I prefer my egg with the white well cooked but the yolk still a bit runny, so I can dunk my bread in it. That's what I always used to do at Slimane's café over at the Goutte d'Or, when I first arrived in Paris. We had eggs every day. Back then, I had the most handsome moustache in the hostel, I was proud, you know . . . I'd like to go back and see Slimane. As soon as I can, I'll go and visit him in his café, soon, inshallah! But I'll wait for my new moustache. If Slimane sees me like this, he'll make fun of me. Slimane used to smoke at least two packets of Gitanes a day, so he'll light up a Gitane and he'll laugh at me, he'll say: "Without his moustache, Mr Moustafa Galbi is dead!" Listen to that ass of a son still cackling away, he's making fun of his father, has he no shame? Tell him to be quiet or I'll cut his head off, I'll take my Opinel and give him the Kabyle smile.'

The Boss is sad, but tomorrow he won't remember this whole scene about his moustache. Instead, he'll probably tell me all over again all about the first time he went to the cinema in Paris.

He and his friends Lakhdar and Mohamed used to have a laugh sneaking in, entering via the emergency exits to avoid paying for their seats. It was the cool thing to do at the time. Or so the Boss says.

He used to spend all his free time there. He liked American films, westerns, Robert Mitchum . . . He wanted to be an actor too, or a musician or something like that. In the seventies, he used to play the guitar for the crowd in old Slimane's famous café at the Goutte d'Or and he'd go by the name of Sam. I guess he was a bit of a hit. Now and then, when he's in the mood, he still sings a little but all that's far behind him now . . .

The next day I wake up feeling tired. I didn't get enough sleep because I spent half the night comforting Linda who'd been having a 'talk' with her boyfriend. The kind of *big talk* that ends up getting really messy, like carnage. Even though they've been together for five years and engaged for several months, the guy explains that he's still not sure about his feelings for her, that he isn't ready to sign up. Which is totally stupid of him . . . I know what Linda's like, and she's a real grudge-bearer, she'll make him pick up the tab on this, big time. Sometimes, it's better to keep your doubts to yourself and pray they'll go away.

Linda's been in love with Issam since secondary school, she sees herself staying with him for the rest of her life, she can picture him being the father of her children, she fantasises about hand-washing his socks and boxers with 'delicates' fabric softener, and up until now, she's always had this blind trust in him. A mistake, if you ask me.

'Fucking bastard! Totally crazy, talking to me about "signing up" like that. What's he playing at? Hello, I'm not some phone company! Signing up, yeah right, who did he think he was going out with – Orange or SFR?'

I don't think it's really sunk in yet, she's too angry for now.

Linda works at Body Boom, a beauty salon that does body treatments and waxing. Seeing as she was edgy today, she got a few complaints from her clients.

She told me she made some girl cry this afternoon. This kid comes in to get her *chnek* waxed, asks for a Brazilian, but Linda's head's somewhere else and she gives her a wonky one. It made me laugh, Linda says it looked more like a Nike *Swoosh* than a Brazilian.

I reckon she needs to get it out of her system, take advantage of this sticky patch in her relationship to let her hair down. She even suggests driving over to Club Tropical on Saturday evening. Now she's talking my language, it means we're going to have a good time. Club Tropical is a one-off as discos go, you have to see it to believe it. When we go there with the girls, it's just to have a laugh. Forget about a classy night out or chatting anyone up. Too many plonkers, plus the vibe is exotic-provincial, but it's something you've got to experience at least once in your life. The DJ, Patrick-Romuald, is a thirty-something from Martinique with an accent fresh from the coconut tree, and his own special way of getting us in the mood. He does a commentary for every track and he's big on motivating the crowd.

'Come on, all you man dems, it's time to SHAKE THAT BUMPER! Go and find your lady friends and invite those sugarbabes to dance! I'm your host on this very special evening, Patrick-Romuald's the name, but you can call me the sharp-toothed croc, and believe me I LIKE to BITE the BUTTS of those WIFEYS . . . *Phwoooaarr*, let's hear it from Fort-de-France! It's going to be a night to remember, with lots of bump 'n' grind action!'

If you ask Patrick-Romuald why his bashes at Club Tropical close at 4 a.m. and not 6 a.m. like most club nights, he gives you this leery grin and says:

'Club Tropical ain't nothing like *most club nights*, and if Patrick-Romuald likes to end his bash at 4 a.m., it's coz if a bredrin ain't found him a wifey to take back to his yard by four in the morning, then he's a wasteman! And if he's found her after four, then he don't wanna dance no more coz he got him one or two other ting on his mind . . .'

Now all I've got to do is persuade Nawel to unglue herself from Mouss, her suction-pad boyfriend – I mean, he's OK and all that, but he's a bit clingy-sticky for my tastes. You never get one without the other, they're more like a pair of socks than a couple.

Mouss is THE good-looking guy on Uprising Estate, everyone's had a crush on him. When he passes by, the girls get their claws out, tear off their knickers, smash the furniture. One smile, one look from him, and there's a crowd of female fans at his feet, he's got more pulling power than the Beatles, more than Claude François, more even than Patrick Sabatier. You need guts to take on a guy like that and not be scared off by the competition. Nawel was hardcore, she even fought Sabrina Achour for him. Now, when you take into account the criminal record and general heftiness of the brute Achour, you'll realise this was serious proof of Nawel's love for Mouss. I hope she'll be up for Club Tropical and won't suddenly pull the stay-at-home wifey on a Saturday evening.

Apeshit

I spent the afternoon round at Auntie Mariatou's.
She gave me cane-rows, American-style, with the plaits
criss-crossing on top of my head. I often ask her for
this hairdo, mainly since I saw the Alicia Keys video
on MTV, that one where she's playing the piano with
her eyes closed and singing for her guy who's banged
up. While Auntie was doing my hair, we were watching
this programme on telly about a couple torn apart
by jealousy, and her running commentary was price-
less, I laughed till my face hurt. So, the guy's called
Tony and his wife is Marjorie. Tony is tall, handsome,
fit and fond of his mum. Marjorie is short and round,
she stutters, she's got hang-ups, and she's very, very
jealous. She checks her guy's text messages, calls him
every few minutes when he's out with his mates, and
if the two of them are walking in the street together
she's always making sure he's not eyeing up any other
girls, meaning the ones who aren't short and round
with a stutter and hang-ups. And if he's unlucky
enough to get caught looking at another woman,
then bam, it's the drama of the century, scandal in

the street, bloodbath. The next part of the programme was a piece to camera, each of them explaining how angry and upset they felt, tears at the ready.

Auntie was living this programme 100 per cent. In fact, she got so worked up she was yanking my hair like a wild thing, I thought she'd end up scalping me. She was talking to Tony like he was in front of her.

'Are you out of your mind sticking with a crazy woman like her? She's sick in the head! Are you a man or what? Leave her to stew, a handsome young man like you, if you walked out on her tomorrow you'd find yourself a better woman, and in a flash . . . Oooooh, now he's going back to her, this is getting serious, tut-tut . . . He's a victim, that guy, and you know what they say: "The lizard has the toughest tail, because the more you chop off, the more it grows back."'

So we were in the middle of this highbrow cultural debate, when Papa Demba darted into the flat. He rushed over to the bookcase in the living room, pounced on a dictionary and started turning the pages like a man possessed. Caught off guard, Auntie and me watched him out of the corners of our eyes. He kept licking his finger and riffling through the pages, frowning like his life depended on whatever definition he was looking up.

In next to no time he'd made Auntie's blood pressure rise. She got so worked up she couldn't help asking what his frantic search was all about.

'What's making you leap on that dictionary like a hare on the run? What are you looking for?'

'I'm looking up the word "gibbon"!' he said, pronouncing the mysterious word with great care.

'Gibbon?'

'Yes, that's right.'

'*Starfoullah!* Why on earth? What's got into you?'

'I was stopped by the police this afternoon, on the main square in Vitry, they wanted to see my ID, nothing new there, a routine check, whatever . . . So anyway, when they decided to let me go again, they were laughing among themselves and saying: "Off you go, gibbon!" I just want to know what they were talking about, it's not a word I'm familiar with.'

'So, what does it mean?'

'Hold on, I'm only up to F.'

He didn't want to read out the whole definition. 'A species of anthropoid monkey from Asia with a broad black face and no tail, it's long powerful arms make it agile when climbing trees . . .'

Papa Demba closed the dictionary of the French language with a sigh that communicated plenty of stories in a similar vein.

Then he left the room. Auntie Mariatou called out: 'Well, there you go, a lot of fuss about nothing. You've got yourself all hot and bothered for a silly remark . . . And what did he gain by listening to such nonsense, can someone tell me?'

'I gained nothing just like I lost nothing,' Papa Demba answered from the other end of the flat. 'I'd have expected something more sophisticated from them, that's all!'

The gibbon in question is a maths teacher at a college in Vitry-sur-Seine, and he gets stopped rather too often in my opinion. When the Feds ask Papa Demba where he's just come from, he says the college because he's a teacher. And that's when they try to play it smart, by adding: 'PE?'

Auntie Mariatou went to find Papa Demba. 'Now listen up! Mr Demba N'Diaye, teacher, son of Diénaba N'Diaye and Yahia N'Diaye, you're the glory of the village of Mbacké, and it's beneath you to take to heart a word you learnt from a pink face in a blue cap! Don't listen to them, *kou yinkaranto*!'

I like it when she gets on her high horse. She said all this with one hand on her waist and the other one busily hoiking up her *boubou*. She looked like one of the characters in that TV comedy *Les Guignols d'Abidjan*, which Auntie loves watching. Then she put on some music (Prince, it's what Auntie listens to all the time) and finished off doing my hair at a furious speed.

I'm at the Café des Histoires at the moment, which is just beyond the Porte de Choisy. I only went in because I liked the name. I brought my notebook with me and sat down on the banquette at the back, like Linda and Nawel always do. I ordered a *café serré* from the nice waitress and borrowed a biro off her. I've never kept a diary because it seems like a stupid ego-trip. I'd rather make up stories, at least they're more fun to read back.

It turns out quite a lot of people write. Even Linda,

when she's fuming. The day she found out her guy had cheated on her, she wrote at least fifteen pages, it was called 'Two-Timed Girl You Don't Mess With'. She nearly lost it that day, I was really worried about her. Then she tore the whole lot up and we never talked about it again. If I was to mention it now, I think she'd be ashamed.

The nice waitress, who I find out later is called Josiane, serves my *café serré* with the kind of smile that makes you want to come back even if the black stuff tastes foul. What am I so focused on writing, she wants to know. So I make up a whole life story for myself, imagining I'm somebody important, just to see what effect it has on a total stranger. I want to know what it feels like to seem intriguing to other people, and I choose Josiane as the guinea pig for my stupid experiment.

'Are you studying?'

'Not at all . . .'

'Oh, OK. So what is it you're writing there?'

'I write short stories that get published every week in a magazine.'

'Really? That's great . . . What kind of short stories? Love stories? Romantic thrillers? Because that's what I'm into reading, I know all of Pierre Bellemare's books almost off by heart . . . And every Wednesday I buy *The Detective*, you might know it, it's full of sordid stories, murders, rapes, kids locked in cupboards. If you'd like to browse, I've got the last ten issues on the bar. My boss wants me to move them because he says it might give our customers the wrong idea, but people ask for them, they're really into them. And like I say, the customers you find propping up the bar, well, they're often the ones without much conversation, so it gives them something to chat about. Don't you think?'

'Yes, yeah, I'm sure you're right, er . . .'

'Oh, call me Josiane! I'm Josiane Vittani and I've been doing this job for at least ten years. Everyone knows me round here.'

'Well, I'm Stéphanie Jacquet, but my byline is Jacqueline Stéphanet, it's so I can stay anonymous.'

'Pleased to meet you, Stéphanie,' and she holds out a hand all decked out with rings.

'Delighted to meet you, Josiane!'

'So, if they're not love stories or thrillers, then what are they?'

'More like social stories, I guess. Stories about people who are up against it, because society hasn't given them a choice, but they try to come out the other side and taste happiness anyway.'

'And people are interested in that kind of stuff?'

Good question, Josiane. I hope so, really I do. I should have come clean and told you I was writing stories about love, harmony and betrayal. At least you can be sure people are interested in that kind of stuff. But the story I want to write looks something like this:

The year is 1960, and it's a sunny afternoon. A MAN comes looking for a WOMAN. They've arranged to meet.

While he's parking his Vespa, she's spying on him from the bathroom window and whispering to herself: 'He's so handsome!' She powders her nose one last time before going down to join him. He's thrilled to see her, he's missed her terribly these last few days, the stain on his jeans is a giveaway. They kiss passionately. Then they climb onto his Vespa and head off. A gentle breeze strokes their faces as they tell each other how madly in love they are.

When they reach the roundabout in front of the shopping centre, ANOTHER MAN intercepts them. Immediately, from his closed face, we can tell he's the villain of the piece. He says something like: 'Hey! You two! Stop!' The woman looks worried sick and says lines to the effect of: 'Oh! Shit! Bloody hell! It's my bastard brother!' And then a terrible fight breaks out between the brother and the man, the gloves are off, they use the most mean, low, down-and-dirty, underhand punches . . .

The brother suddenly lunges for the man's neck and says to him: 'Listen up, you son of a bitch, this is the last time I ever want to see you sniffing around my little sister, get it?' Then he turns to his poor sister: 'As for you, slut! I never want you going out with another black Muslim illegal immigrant, who's an unemployed orphan with a criminal record, again, d'you hear me? Or I'll kill you, you bitch!' She tries to stand up for herself: 'But I love him!' 'I don't give a shit!'

the thug-brother comes back at her. So the two lovers are separated by the evil militant National Front brother, but the man is undaunted and in love and he vows to win back his beauty . . .

The moral of the story has to be something really dumb, like love has no colour or religion or social-security numb . . . I've disappeared inside my own bubble and I've thoroughly enjoyed myself. Josiane gives me an espresso on the house and invites me to come back any time. I think the Café des Histoires will become my HQ. I'll go back there with the note-book I jacked from Leclerc, or my girlfriends, or maybe even with Tonislav if he decides to call me. If you'd told me that one day I'd fall for an illegal Yougo with a silver tooth, I'd never have believed it . . .

No Point Running, if You Want to Catch a Cheetah

'Where are you going?'

'Out.'

'Don't disrespect me, I can see you're going out, so stop being a smart-arse. Answer my question, Foued, where are you going?'

'Down to the basement to go on the PlayStation with the others. I'll be back in half an hour –'

'And who's the "others"?'

''Low it, man, you're getting me vexed. The "others" means the same old: Abdullah, Bensaïd, Hassan, plus Nikolas and Tomas, AKA the Villo brothers. Why're you coming down heavy? They don't have to answer to nobody.'

'I've already told you I don't like you hanging out with them, they're poisoning you, they're the wrong kind of crowd, they're stupid and you'll turn out even worse –'

'Their mum says the same thing about me.'

'Piss off then, and I hope it's not to go and watch those dirty DVDs, you're disgusting, you lot.'

'*Wotever.* I don't need to go down to the basement for that, I've got a telly in my bedroom, if I want to give myself a –'

'Urggh! Go on, move it! Get out! Spare me the details, you little pig. You think you've grown wings just because you've turned sixteen? Don't forget you wet your bed till you were eight, and that's only half of sixteen! And don't forget who cleaned up your little piss-covered *swizzle stick* back in the day either!'

That made him leg it like a nutter across the hallway and pull on a pair of trainers, bursting into an evil cackle. This piece of shit was laughing at the idea I might feel disgusted by him, and he jetted off clutching his shoot-em-ups and his football games. Still, there's no risk of me feeling genuinely disgusted by my only brother, who I raised from a little baby. Then again, the older he gets, the more I want to slap that *chétane* every morning. Plus, he really goes all out because he knows what a charmer he is. Foued's a handsome guy, there's no denying it, with his smooth dark skin, his wicked black eyes, good teeth, a compact body that's buff for his age and, the golden rule with him, winter and summer, his hair shaved almost to a number one. When I ask him why he doesn't let it grow a bit, he says:

'If I let my hair grow, it looks rank, man. With this frizzy Arab wig, you'd think I'd got an old carpet on my head! It's for my street cred, innit.'

For his sixteenth birthday, I let him get his ear pierced, but only after he'd banged on about it. He wanted it bad, that's for sure. He didn't come home so late, his marks picked up at school and sometimes he even did the washing-up for me.

'D'you want me to do the dusting, Ahlème?'

'Ahlème who?'

'Ahlème my sister who I love with all my heart.'

'More . . .'

'The nicest, cleverest, cutest girl on the whole of Uprising Estate!'

'OK, that's enough, you were doing all right until you went over the top there, you don't want to be taking the piss. Well, if you're prepared to shove your pride up your bumper, then I guess you really do want your ear pierced.'

'Yeah, I want it and I'm gonna have it!'

'Well, you're certainly sure of yourself . . .'

'I mean, if my darling sister gives me the green light, of course.'

'That's more like it . . .'

So I ended up giving in. Reluctantly, but I gave in. I had to hand it to him, he deserved it for trying so hard. The day he came back home with the diamond in his ear, I'll be honest, I didn't take it so well. I found it hard to swallow. It bugs me my little brother looks like all those other R 'n' B singers who are basically a lot less masculine than me.

But I wouldn't give in on everything. Foued wanted us to go to Leclerc together so that I'd buy him one of those blond hair dyes in the L'Oréal Excellence Cream range. No way, little bro. I'd rather he got a scorpion tattoo on his abs like Joey Starr, I'd find that less traumatic.

He takes good care of himself, the little jerk. Mornings are hell, he's got this whole ritual going down, rushes straight for the bathroom, spends hours in there. He throws all his pocket money and EMA grant on garms and lotions. I keep telling him he should be ashamed for a bloke of his age. My brother's generation is the 'guy-lite' generation, which in their language translates as nice-smelling, buff-looking guys . . . And it's not just Foued who's a *lite*, all his crowd are *lites* too. Their motto is: 'Lite and nothin' else'. And when they walk past the girls, the *wifeys* as they call them, they get a kick out of strutting their stuff, and the girls can't get enough of it: 'Wow, he's like *lite*, and he smells niiice!' which only puffs up the boys' super-inflated egos.

My brother is such a show-off, I could thump him sometimes. Wanting to dye his hair blond was too much for me. I was full of the psycho-babble in those books Nawel lends me now and then, so I told him that if he didn't know who he was any more, if he was having strange feelings that he didn't understand, we could always talk about it. He giggled and went: 'Don't worry, I'm not a poof, if that's what you're thinking.'

Bleached hair's been the craze for a few years now. One whiff of summer and you see all these blond heads popping up out of nowhere, like a brood of fluffy chicks strutting around these endz. It can look 'fresh-groovy-smooth', but it can also scare the little kids. It's kind of double-edged. I'm worried that Foued will turn into a real heart-breaker later on.

He's my little brother, and I've brought him up and everything, but I reckon he'll be a right bastard when it comes to girls. That's how I'm feeling it. The phone's been ringing a lot recently, and I'm always getting these little slappers who want to speak to him.

Today, even though I didn't sign up to it, I had to referee a ping-pong match, professional standard, like the ones between those super-quick Chinese players who hit so fast you can barely follow the ball. Two girls called up in turn, it felt like a relay race, except that Foued wasn't in. It didn't take me long to crack – one of them decided to tell me her life story so I told her where to go. Yeah, so I was harsh with her, but she was taking a big fat liberty.

'Sorry, it's Eva again, I already called just a while ago to –'

'Yes, you don't need to tell me, I had noticed. What d'you want this time?'

'Er . . . I wanted to know if Foued was back yet or not?'

'You called ten minutes ago, not even, and I told you he'd be back in about half an hour, yes or no?'

'Er . . . yes.'

'So, if you can count up to thirty, then you can work out he'll be back in about twenty minutes, so perhaps you'd like to stop calling because it's starting to get on my tits.'

'Are you his sister?'

'Yes, that's right, his sister, not his secretary.'

'Does a girl called Vanessa phone your place too?'

'Look, do I ask you questions? We don't know each other, I'm not your friend, we're not even the same age. Do I ask you what colour thong you're wearing? No one called Vanessa rings here and very soon there won't be anyone called Eva either.'

'You don't need to talk to me like that, I won't call again.'

'That's great news, bye.'

I'd forgotten how hideous it was being sixteen. The second slapper phoned a few minutes later. Sure enough, she was called Vanessa. A proper little slapper's name. I hardly gave her time to say who she was before I hung up.

When Foued's out, it's a good excuse for me to tidy his room, because he doesn't exactly appreciate my intrusions into his 'endz', as he calls his bedroom. Fatal mistake. Show me the shit-heap in your bedroom, and I will tell you who you are. Well, I can reliably inform you that Foued is a crazy bastard. Thinking I'd just tidy up a drawer full of random stuff, I landed on these packets of multicoloured condoms. So, Sir was denying himself nothing. Then, sorting out the clothes that were all jumbled up in his wardrobe, I pulled out three bin liners full of women's handbags – Lancaster, Vuitton, Lancel – and that's not the half of it . . . In a shoebox under the bed I found wads of money. Not a couple of notes, not three or ten or twenty. Wads.

I couldn't believe what I'd discovered. I was mown down. There was no way it could be his. Except, of course, it was.

The first idea that flashed into my head was to grab the whole lot, stuff it down the loo and tug on our trusty old chain. As for the bags, I wanted to burn them on the waste ground behind the hill. But that kind of superhero bullshit is what you see in moralistic American films, where honesty wins the day. What we're dealing with here is real life, and in real life I'm not so keen on the idea of my little brother getting shot at. So I decided not to touch anything before I found out what was going on.

I got dinner ready for the Boss, read the newspaper to him, and listened to him talking about the never-ending games of dominoes he used to play round at Lakhdar's when he lived in Rue des Martyrs. The Boss was a talent, he won every time, his combinations just kept getting better. The others were jealous, especially Abdelhamid, who was always trying to figure it out: 'But, Moustafa, what the devil do you do to wipe the table with your opponent every time? Perhaps you've got a special technique you don't want to share with us? Or maybe you've cast a spell on the dominoes at Lakhdar's.' Not a bit of it. The Boss's only technique was trusting to luck. One day, I'd like to follow that philosophy of life, only problem is I don't believe in luck or trust right now. I don't believe in much any more. I believe in Allah, who is my only guide, and in social benefits too, because it's thanks to them I get by.

The Boss fell asleep at last. Things were almost peaceful again.

Foued was out for nearly four hours, and not the 'half-hour' he'd promised me as he headed down to the basement. I'm not even sure if he really did go down to the basement now; to be honest, I'm not really sure about anything any more.

He walks into the flat, cool as you like, whistling the theme tune for a gherkins ad that's on telly a lot at the moment. He doesn't know what he's in for, poor guy, I'm going to make him spit and sizzle like a merguez. I lie in wait for him, sitting on his bed, in the half-light.

'Ahlème! Ahlème! Where are you? Is the Boss asleep?'

He comes into his bedroom, gropes around in the dark and flicks the switch. He jumps, surprised to see me.

'Fuck! Shit my pants! You gave me a scare, man! Wassup? What the fuck are you doing here in the dark?'

I don't answer, I'm just looking at him. I want to get up and tear him to pieces.

'Answer me! What's got into you? You look like you're possessed! *Naâl chétane.*'

I'm up, I grab him by the neck, I pin him to the wall and I shake him furiously like he's a limp rag.

'You little piece of shit! All that crap I've found in your bedroom – where does it come from?'

'What are you talking about? Let go of me! You're sick in the head, man.'

'No, I won't let go! And you can stop fucking with me. You know what I'm talking about, you little shit. The papers in the shoebox, the handbags in the

94

wardrobe! And as for those condoms in your drawer, what's that about?'

He shoves me away, unnerved now. I lose my balance and end up on his bed. I get up and lunge at him again, like a cokehead. I go for his throat so violently that even I'm surprised. I grip his neck tight and start crying with anger.

'I said, where does it come from? Answer me before I kill you! Answer me!'

'Stop it! Please, stop it! You're hurting me –'

'What about me? You don't think I'm hurting here? I kill myself for you, I've done everything for you!'

'I can't breathe, let go . . .'

The Boss wakes up. His voice drags me out of my madness.

'I can't sleep! Turn the television off!'

'Go back to sleep, Dad! It's all right, don't worry, the telly's off!'

I take Foued by the shoulders and push him down so he's sitting on the bed. He feels his neck to check everything's still there, that his head is still attached to his body. I must have really gone for it, he's all red and his eyes are popping out of his face.

'No point getting all vexed like that, I'm telling you, innit. It's not my money, it's the crew's, I just look after it for them, that's all . . . I swear it's not mine, I swear on –'

'What d'you mean, you look after it for them?'

'Well, like, er, that – I look after it for them. They hand it over to me for a few days and then they pick it up again, and in exchange they give me a wodge of papers, fifty euros, something like that . . .'

'Is this some kind of a joke? What about the bags?'

'That's one of the older guys from the crew, he left us this little job to do.'

I sit down next to him – if I stay standing up, I'll die.

'What does a "job" mean? And who are these older guys?'

'It means they pass stuff onto us and we've got to get rid of it, we sell it, innit. Then at the end, they give us some dough. That's how it works.'

'Like with the DVDs?'

'Yes . . .'

'Yes . . . Is that all you've got to say for yourself? Didn't you learn your lesson last time? My God, are you really that dumb? Have you thought about the po-pos? What if you go down? They'll come and search the flat. What are you thinking, you idiot? Those older guys are arseholes, they're using you as a cover, don't you get it? D'you want the Boss to die of a heart attack when the po-pos come round here, is that it? And me too, while we're at it? Fuck . . . I could kill you! It's not like you don't have everything you need, is it?'

'It's no big deal, it's OK. You don't know the older guys. Don't call them arseholes, you're judging them when you don't even know them!'

'Who are they? What are their names?'

'You don't know them, drop it!'

'Spit out their tags, I'm telling you!'

'Fizz, Cockroach, Poison, Blade, Leper, Magnum,

they're just older guys you don't know . . . They're family and this is the ghetto, innit.'

'Oh right, so they're your family, you bastard – is that what you're fucking saying?'

'Stop crying, please . . .'

'Bawling my eyes out is the only thing I've got left to do, I'm going crazy here . . . Don't you ever stop and think? Don't you use that thing God put in your head for a brain? Did you honestly think I'd never find out about any of this?'

'Fuck it, what about me? You don't think I want to bawl too, sometimes? Even if I make out like it's no big deal, it's only because I don't want you worrying about me, that's all. Just because I can eat and sleep, it doesn't mean everything's fine. This is the street, that's how it is. I'm not the only one, and anyway, I'm not doing nothing, man, compared to the others –'

'But you're not the others! I don't give a fuck about the others –'

'Don't you get it? I've had it with seeing you work like a dog. Always running around everywhere to scrape the money together. You know the clothes I wear? Well, I lied to you about them, nobody gave them to me, and the truth is nobody "lent" me the telly in my bedroom either, and that PlayStation doesn't belong to Jimmy, it's mine. All that stuff's mine. I paid for it with MY money –'

'And you don't feel ashamed?'

'No, I don't feel ashamed! You've got to look out for yourself, that's what everyone does here. You don't see that. You think you know everything that's going on, but you don't know anything! Plus you're a girl, so it's not the same.'

'That's got nothing to do with it.'

'It's got everything to do with it! You don't understand, it's the jungle out there. You gotta fuck 'em up the arse before they fuck you. The ones on top, the rich kids, they're the lions, and we're the hyenas, all we get are the leftovers –'

'SHUT YOUR MOUTH! THAT'S NOT TRUE! STOP IT! Are those older guys filling your head with this shit? And you swallow it like an idiot? Just because they've pissed on their own lives, doesn't mean they can piss on the younger ones' chances. Those bastards want you to think the game's already over. Yes, all right, so we do have to fight twice as hard as the rest. I know that, so stop thinking you can teach me about life. Who do you think you are? I'd never have thought you'd be so easily led . . . And school? What's school all about?'

''Low it, man, you know it's a load of bollocks. You left when you were sixteen, so stop giving me a hard time. As for the older guys, not even the ones who went to school can get a J.O.B.'

'D'you want to end up in *habs* or what? Because if you carry on like this and that's your goal, you're bang on target, you'll get your place in the slammer, no worries. So how do I get by, hey? I keep my nose to the grindstone and I keep myself out of the shit. What you're doing is a cop-out. You're weak. Your money stinks. You're going to hand everything back. Hand back the dough and tell the older guys you don't want to do it any more. And if *you* won't tell them, then I'll find them and I'll tell them myself. D'you hear me? You know me, I mean it when I say I'll go and see them, I've got balls, so it'll be better for you if you go yourself!'

'I can't do that, no way –'

'You're *going* to do it! It's non-negotiable!'

'I'll be in shit!'

'You'll be in even bigger shit if you don't do it. And what about those condoms? What kind of crazy stuff are you up to?'

'That's completely different, it's my life. When you've got a guy, I don't say anything to you!'

'I'm not the same age as you, remember! You're still a fucking kid, you're just a little shit-head. D'you want to get one of your little slappers preggo? Is that the plan?'

'I'm careful.'

'Yeah, right . . . With all your filthy money you could at least have bought yourself a mobile, then they'd stop pissing me off by calling here.'

'I've got one.'

'Great, thanks for the news update . . . That fucking tops the lot, that does. Nice one! So you've taken me for an idiot from start to finish! I'm out of here, I don't want to see your face. I'm going to my room, it's better that way. I'd never have believed it, that I can't bear to look at my own brother any more –'

'Stop pretending you're my mum. You're not my mum!'

'SHUT IT! SHUT THE FUCK UP!'

I couldn't stop myself from giving him the slap of his life, the final whack, the ultimate blow. I hit him with all my soul, with everything I had left in me. I nearly flipped open his sunroof, a bit more and his head would have flown off.

I couldn't look him in the eye after that. I just went into my room, totally out of it. I lay down on my bed without even bothering to put on my pyjamas because I wanted to fall asleep fast and for the longest time.

That's when this song by IAM came into my head, I used to listen to it all the time nearly ten years ago now:

> Little bro's left the playground, can barely walk and
>   he wants seven-league boots.
> Little bro wants to grow up too fast, he's forgetting
>   there's no point running, Little bro . . .

Yeah, no point running, 'especially when you're trying to catch a cheetah', as my dear Auntie Mariatou would say.

On the Down-Low

I went round to Auntie's feeling rinsed out. Like an old mop. I must have looked in a right state, sobbing and blurting out the story to her. She made me a coffee using the percolator Papa Demba gave her for her birthday – ever since she got that gadget, she's been fixing coffees all day long. She insisted I calm down and take some deep breaths, because I looked like a Kenyan at the end of a marathon.

Auntie was gobsmacked when I told her about the fight, she couldn't believe it. At one point, I even suggested sending Foued back to the *bled* for a reality check, but obviously that was a stupid idea.

'It won't work, he doesn't even know the country, you can't let him discover it as punishment. And you haven't set foot there for well over ten years, have you?'

'Yeah . . . You're right. I don't know what to do any more. When all this acting up started, I thought it was a phase. No big deal, just his age. But he's already chasing after money. I just don't get it.'

'If he carries on like this and gets caught by the police, they won't give him an easy ride, he's not a minor any more. Have you heard about the "double penalty"?'

'I know, Auntie. What does my head in is he doesn't click. He can't see what he's landing himself in. He's after too much dough.'

'Come on, he's caught in a vicious circle, that's all. You mustn't give up on him. Get behind him. Talk to him.'

'He's not stupid. He's a nice kid, my brother, but he wants to be a *man dem*, he wants to be rich. And I can talk to him 'til I'm blue in the face, it won't make any difference. The more he gets, the more he'll want.'

'As we say in Africa, "Money rings in money".'

'I swear –'

'Money rings in money, but the rich ring the police.'

She managed to get a smile out of me. Just then, her daughter Wandé came into the living room clutching her class book neatly covered in brown paper.

'Ahlème, please can you help me with my French homework? The verbs are like this big problem . . .'

Auntie was quick to react, seeing as I was in no fit state.

'Go to your bedroom and get on with your home-work yourself! Don't you think we've got enough problems, without you adding to them?'

For the rest of the evening, Auntie tried to talk me out of going down to the basement to speak with the older guys. It's not my style to fold my arms and wait for the rain, but at the same time she's not wrong, it wouldn't be smart to get involved.

Once I'm feeling calmer, I thank Auntie for always being there for me and I head out. I'm like a beggar with my flip-flops from the market and my flimsy dress, the one I wear instead of pyjamas, that's ripped at the thigh. My head's killing me. My eyes are red and puffy, you'd think I'd drunk litres of alcohol. I'm staggering like a soak.

Of course, instead of going home, I head down.

I make straight for Block 30, the high-risk area in our endz, where most people are too scared to go, and where even the BAC thinks twice about heading if there's some action.

I walk into the dimly lit entrance not sure what I'm doing. Three guys are leaning against the wall. I freeze for a few seconds, I've got no idea what to say to them, or at least no idea where to start. I've only just showed up and the smell of blow is already making me gag, all mixed in with the stench of the place, like an open bin, I'm worried I'm about to puke. The first guy, the one with his head just below the tag that reads 'Fuck Sarko', speaks to me.

'What you lookin' for? What you doin' here?'

'I'm looking for some people.'

'What d'you want?'

'It's about my little brother.'

'Who's that?'

'Foued.'

'The Arab kid, the Orphan?'

'He's called Foued, I said.'

'Who d'you want to see?'

'Magnum, the Leper, Cockroach, whoever . . .'

He's weird, this guy, he looks high and he's sizing me up in this funny way. What was I thinking, rushing over here so late? They're going to get the idea I'm looking for something dodgy.

Just then, one of the guys at the back lowers his hood and comes towards me. When he's under the revolting light of the neon strip, I recognise Didier, the ice-cream seller's son, this guy who I grew up with, who I cheated at school with, who I used to steal from supermarkets with, who I even had my first snog with. I'm stunned. He looks kind of taken aback too.

'No way! Back in the day, man, innit! Ahlème the Bullet! What the shit are you doing here?'

'What the shit are you doing here? I haven't seen you in the longest time.'

'I went down, innit.'

What's happening to me in this block is like a crap TV script, except it's for real. So then he glues me this kiss on the cheek, full of brotherhood and happy memories. It's getting kind of awkward, I don't know how to tackle the problem any more.

'D'you know this weirdo, Cockroach?'

'Yeah, yeah, I know her, no worries.'

Like it wasn't obvious. And another thing, I hate people talking about me in front of me like that.

'So you're the one they call Cockroach?'

'Yeah.' He looks down, embarrassed.

'Straight up . . . and when people call you "Cockroach", you answer?'

'Er, yeah . . . dunno.'

'Where d'you get the tag?'

He starts sniggering and the others snigger too. One of them asks Didier for some Rizlas. He gets two out of his pocket and hands them over, a bit sheepish in front of me.

'Cockroach, it's like this joke, man, you get me, it's been my tag since bare times . . . Coz these bastards, like one day we were pissin' around and this tiny cockroach comes outta my jacket, you get me. It's the flats in our endz, man . . . since they stopped sending those guys who like spray stuff everywhere, there's bare cockroaches, I'm telling you. So that's how it started, you get me . . . But it don't mean I got insects coming outta my pockets, I'm not grimy, innit, it's just bare jokez. They've got their ghetto tags too: he's Stray Dog, and the other guy over there, he's Escobar.'

'Escobar? Because of Pablo Escobar?'

'Yeah, that's right, except it's more like . . . Basically, his real name's Alain, and he's full of bullshit!' he laughs. 'See, it kind of mashes the legend! Alain, bro!'

'Fuck your family, dickhead, look who's talking, you scum, with a name like Didier!' the other guy hits straight back.

'Yeah, but Alain's worse! And your mum's called Bertha, innit.'

'Shut your gob, I don't talk about your mum, 'low it, man –'

'He's right, it's worse! For real!'

The other bloke, who's kept out of it 'til now, starts shit-stirring.

'As for you, Mouloud, don't even go there, with your grocer's tag.'

'Up yours.'

'Nah, up yours.'

'Er . . . sorry, Didier, but can I talk to you about something?'

We head outside, away from the others. It's a chilly night. I'm hardly wearing anything, and I'm shivering.

'Don't be scared . . . wassup?'

'I'm not scared.'

Tonight, it's not Cockroach I'm talking to but Didier. I explain the whole situation to him, in words that are easy to understand, with just the right amount of anger and indignation. I tell him how worried I am and how frightened too, I tell him how me and my brother have to tiptoe around this *bled*, have to stay off the radar, because we weren't born here. He must have heard the stories about people being kicked out. It's true what people say, it's not just some urban myth. If Foued doesn't lie low from now on, the pigs won't show him any mercy. And this big speech I'm making isn't just for my brother. I'm asking Didier and his bredrins not to ruin other kids' lives the way they've ruined their own. I know I'm not going to change the system, that's how it is in our endz, but fuck it, Foued's only sixteen.

Didier isn't a complete piece of shit. He's done some shitty things, for sure, but pieces of shit don't hang out in the lobby of Block 30. No, the real bastards, in their comfy armchairs, decide *who*'s going to hang out in the lobby of Block 30. They're the

106

ones who can decide to kick a guy like Foued out of France for one screw-up too many. Even Didier can understand that. He used to have desires, dreams, stuff like that . . . He probably doesn't remember telling me about it, but back when his dad used to slip us Italian ice creams behind the other kids' backs, he wanted to work on boats, the ones with white sails. Except Didier didn't think he'd ever get to work on boats because, at Ivry, there's no sea.

When we get down to the nitty-gritty, I realise he's involved in all the scams my brother's mixed up in. He apologises, says on his mum's life how sorry he is, promises he didn't know Foued was my brother. Are these empty words? I'm wondering. Maybe it's just the spliff talking. But deep down, I believe him.

'You're right, we'll keep your bro well away from what's going down. Guaranteed, innit. I'll watch out for him. Everyone knows who I am round here, and don't worry, they listen. You don't mess with Cockroach. I'm even here for you too, if you need anything. I'll keep an eye on him, I swear on my family's life, you've got my word, Ahlème. Nobody'll give him any shit, nobody'll get him mixed up in stuff. Sorry. I didn't know you were the Orphan's sister –'

'And stop calling him the Orphan, he's got a name.'

'Yeah, but it's butterz, innit . . . all right, 'low it man, sorry.'

I head off, dying of cold. We've agreed I'll come back tomorrow at the same time, to bring Didier the money and the rest of that crap stashed at my place. I give him a big warm thank-you, and I thank God too, I give Him thanks for letting me deal with Didier instead of that dodgy guy who goes by the name of Escobar, because he would have demanded payback, for sure, he'd have asked me to do something rank for keeping Foued safe from the crew's dirty biz. I'll do anything for my brother, no matter what it takes, so I'm glad I wasn't put to the test.

Running Out of Steam

The phone rang. I knew it was Tonislav as soon as I picked up. His 'hello' was like a magic spell or, better, a blessing. He said to meet at Châtelet Les Halles by the fountain, in the Place Carré. For the first time in my life, I get what 'needing somebody' might mean. But why him? No idea. I'm losing my grip, just thinking about seeing him makes my heart race at ten thousand an hour . . . My knees are wobbly, and I feel like a clueless teenager on her first date. I must look like such an idiot.

In the RER, on my way to see him, I'm thinking I'll just blag it. My plan's something like this, jump on his neck and ask him to hold me very tight, even if he's so shocked he never calls me again. I don't know why, but today I feel like giving in to the kind of stuff you wouldn't normally catch me dead doing. I'll let him see all the weaknesses that I kill myself trying to hide from the rest of the world, and most of all from me. Too bad if he flips out. It'd just mean he's a jerk like all the others and he wasn't worth it anyway. I'm not wearing my cris garms this time. I'm just me, and I don't care any more.

When I get to the Place Carré, I sit down on the steps near to the fountain. I'm on time but I can't see him.

There's bare peeps in this place. It's weird being in the middle of all this fizz, taking it in like I'm not here. I watch the people passing by, running, strolling. I've got this strange feeling that everyone is happy except for me. It's like they're alive, living life to the full, slap bang in my face with their happiness, no shame. Of course, I know it's not for real, but that doesn't make it any easier convincing myself. It's like all these people have so many dreams I'll never be let in on. They stroll around, they flaunt it. I know what they're trying to do, they want to rub it in 'til I'm fuming. Well, they've won.

At this moment in time, I feel like I've lost at dice. You throw the dice onto the carpet dozens of times, and each time you really believe it's going to happen. You can already see it landing with the glorious six face up, but nothing doing, it's always a low score instead. One, two or three tops, never more. No matter how hard you shake it in your hands, blow on it, close your eyes and whisper a prayer, it's always the same. I reckon after so many defeats, you've got the right to be disappointed.

I feel like a child who's being punished. I'm in the corner of the Place Carré and I want just one thing: to see this stranger appear, and for me to bury myself in his arms. I'm losing the plot big time, this is getting ova-wack.

A group of Mexican musicians set up in the square. They start with the sound system, before moving on to last-minute fine-tunings. They're just a few metres away from me, and they're hilarious with their gigantic sombreros. Listening to them might distract me a bit. It's not hard guessing what they're about to play. Generally speaking, it always kicks off with 'Guantanamera'. Once they've played the first few notes, I recognise the tune and go *result*. A few happy people gather round, partly blocking my view, while I'm still waiting impatiently for this baddy who's making me want him big time . . .

The worst is I can't get hold of him, he hasn't got a phone. Each time he's called me, it was from a phone box. It sucks not being in control of anything. This guy doesn't realise it but he's holding my puppet strings. Normally, I've got no time for people who are late, but here I am waiting for him. I keep trying to cheer myself up, with: 'OK, come on, I'm out of here, I'm not a victim who waits thirty years for a guy I hardly know, that fries my brain!' But I don't get up. I stay fixed to the spot like a rusty old nail. During this excruciating wait, I lose count of the number of people, including kids who aren't even over eighteen, bugging the shit out of me, asking for a light, telling me how fit I look, wondering if I've got a minute for us to get to know each other . . .

And I answer them cynically, right from the gut: 'No, I haven't got a light, and I might look fit on the outside but I've got HIV on the inside, still interested?' or 'If you think you can get to know me in a minute, I can't look that interesting . . .'

And then, I see a familiar figure through the crowd, some way off. He starts running. He was just late, that was all, well, an hour late . . . I'm starting to have serious doubts about our story: I've been here on my own, for nearly an hour, waiting for him in a complete state, and then, when I do see him coming, I don't even feel like giving him a hard time or making a scene. I just want him to hold me tight with all the passion in the world. So maybe I've watched too many films on telly, but who cares, I've got him and I never want to let go of him again. He's even closer now and I'm up, like a starving person reaching out for a crust of bread, and I walk in his direction inspired by the most romantic 'here comes the bride' moments in the movies. For all I know, this man's a remorseless criminal, an assassin, a rapist, a ripper, or a guy who butchers his victims to steal a kidney and sell it on via the Internet . . . But I head towards him with a big smile on my face, my arms held out and my heart his for the taking. It's then, at that precise moment, that I realise for the first time: I'm in love with this stranger, I'm putty in his hands.

I don't need to take the lead, he just puts his comforting arms around me and holds me tight, squeezing not too much, not too little, just tight, the way I imagined it. He smells of musk, his hair's gelled back, one lock falls on his forehead, I can feel his warm breath on my neck . . . it's enough to make me dizzy. It's like he knew exactly what I needed from him.

Our afternoon together was surreal. If he hadn't had to leave, I could happily have spent the evening with him, maybe the night too, or my whole life. He read my palm and made up a life for me. If you ask me, I don't reckon he can read palms any more than he can read feet. But I let him carry on all the same, it was nice, it tickled.

And then, just before we had to go our separate ways, he took off his silver chain and put it round my neck. I kissed him to thank him for his present and I meant it 100 per cent. After that, he told me I was a princess and deserved to be treated like one.

It was very cute, but I just found myself thinking: 'Nice one, sweetheart, but try telling that to the silly cow at the jobcentre, the old bag at the family bene-fits centre or that fat dumpling I had for a boss last week on my temping "assignment" at the Paris Bakery, I'm not sure they'd all agree with you.'

He left too quickly for my liking, but promised to call me the next day, and I believed him, no ques-tions asked, I didn't even feel tempted to let out my famous 'Yeah, right, whatever', like I've done with every other boyfriend. I was on a cloud . . . God, please, let me stay here a bit longer.

Comings and Goings

Ever since she made up with Issam, Linda's gone off the scene, she's scarcer than a solar eclipse. As for Nawel, it's like she's more glued to her *gadjo* than ever before. I talk to them on the phone, because they still want to hear my news, but I get the feeling they're distancing themselves. We don't really do stuff together any more. The small amount of cash I manage to put to one side, I'll blow on the Boss's physio sessions, because he's been complaining a lot about backache these last few days. Too bad, I tell myself, I'd rather the girls had a nice time, enjoyed the good weather without me. Plus I don't like it if they're on a guilt trip every time they're out with me, feeling bad about spending their money and worrying they're just rubbing it in, even if they never stop offering to help out.

As for Foued, we're kind of back on speaking terms since that whole mess-up. He goes through the motions, but I can tell it's just *belâani*. A monosyllable here and there, stupid little things like going to buy the bread, switching TV channels or taking out the rubbish. He doesn't hang about outside so much, I don't think he's having an easy time of it. I guess his bredrins must be pulling faces, not giving him so many ratings because he's been muscled out by the older guys. So he's around at home a lot; he doesn't even play football at Coubertin any more.

This morning, I got a letter from my aunt Hanan. Every time she writes to me, she never stops banging on about how I should come back to Algeria with my brother and the Boss, and she always uses her favourite method: the guilt trip. Back home, it's one of the mainstays of our education.

Your grandmother is old and sick. What are you waiting for? That she leaves without saying goodbye to you? We miss you terribly. Each time we remember you here, the whole household weeps, there are even tears trickling down the walls. Come and see us, so that we can enjoy your company and unite our family at last. Our sister, God bless her soul, left you as orphans, and she would never have wanted us to be separated for such a long time. We're impatient for your return, that great day, inshallah, when we will give sincere thanks before God for our reunion. My older children are all married now, you weren't here for any of their weddings, and they missed you terribly. As for my youngest children, they've grown up without even being able to remember their own cousins. So if God wills it, perhaps this summer, destiny will reunite us.

Please, Ahlème, can you send us a parcel with some medicines for your grandmother, the blue boxes like last time? Because you know all that kind of thing is too expensive here.

May God grant you compassion, dear Ahlème, and you will be rewarded, inshallah. Your cousin Souriya asks if you could think to put two or three bras in, that Playtex brand, the lacy cross-my-hearts please, may God keep you, you know she is getting married soon. Our Kabyle cousins, Sabrina and Razika, the ones who work at the hairdresser's in Ain Temouchent, say hello to you, they'd like you to check out the prices of turbo hairdryers, they promise to reimburse you as soon as they can. As for Naïma, who celebrated her seventeenth birthday last season, she'd like something from you she calls 'thongs', I don't know what this means but she said that you would definitely know and, to finish off, there's just one other thing that I'd like you to send me from France, it's that cream against old age that I asked you for, I think the make is Diadermine. May God preserve and guide you all, may He shower you with all His goodness and may He bring *baraka* into your house. Take good care of your little brother and your poor father.

I wonder if this letter was actually meant for me, or whether she should have sent it directly to Father Christmas. Because basically it looks more like a wish list. Nothing new there. I feel like I don't have much in common with them, apart from a few memories. It all seems so far away.

The day we left, I was wearing a little blue dress Mum had sewn for me. I remember I'd been bugging her to make me one 'that twirls'.

It was Uncle Mohamed who drove us to the airport in Oran. He left us with these air hostesses who were wearing lots of make-up and promised to make sure we got to Paris safely. Then he held me tight. It was only then that it really sunk in, with his beard tickling my neck and him whispering about how I was going to have to be brave. That's when I knew it was going to be tough because, until that day, Uncle Mohamed was too shy and proper to show me any affection whatsoever, apart from giving me a kiss once a year, for the Eid-el-Kebir.

I left my country, and I left a whole chunk of my life behind too. For the last time, I looked up at the sky of Algeria through the plane window, thinking I'd be returning soon. I haven't been back to the *bled* since I got to France and, if I did decide to go back, I don't know how I'd cope with the big homecoming. Recently, though, I've been giving it some serious thought.

Nawel says she might be able to pull a few strings to get me a job in her uncle Abdou's shoe shop, on Boulevard de la Chapelle. He's just sacked his sales assistant because he caught her with a customer in the stockroom. If the word in his ear works, I might actually land a long-term contract and be able to save a bit. Then, I could take the Boss and Foued back to Algeria, to our mother's village, towards Sidi Bel Abbès, to the family home, Dar Mounia.

These days, I'm spending most of my time with the Boss because I'm out of work. I treasure these moments together. I can read his life in the lines of his furrowed face, in his misty eyes, in his drooping eyelids, in the curls of his hair turned white, and I think about how much I'd miss him if he kicked the bucket. When we spend time together, there's give and take on both sides, he tells me his stories and I sing him songs. I listen attentively, and wait for him to have his siesta before I beat it to the Café des Histoires to write down all the tales he's told me. I've become one of the regulars, and it's unusual for me to make something a habit. When I get there, Josiane already knows what I want to drink. She brings me my *café serré* and most of the time, seeing as the place is empty in the afternoons, she joins me at my table. She says I'm a good listener, quick to inspire trust, and that being interested in other people like I am is a wonderful gift.

Trouble is, she still calls me Stéphanie Jacquet and keeps hassling me to bring along the newspapers where my stories get published. I can't bring myself to tell her I took her for a ride.

Josiane never wanted to have children, and when I ask her if she doesn't regret this, her answer's fair enough: 'Forty-eight is a bit late for regrets, plus I know I'm not stable, so if it's a case of having kids when you can't give them a proper family, you're better off not doing it. Anyway, being pregnant completely changes your body . . . I think that had something to do with it as well, I didn't want saggy skin and boobs beyond hope.'

She's pretty, all right, and a big flirt. She's a bit old-skool French sometimes, but I like it. Josiane's on her fourth marriage and she says she's thinking about getting another divorce, although she's not too sure on what grounds. She says there was never any valid motive for her previous divorces either. I think she gets a bit lost in all these relationships. She wanted to keep the name of her first husband, because she thought that Josiane Vittani sounded like a film actress from the sixties. She's funny and she's honest. It's great she's like that at the café, but I reckon it must be weird living with her on a daily basis.

'And another thing, at my age it's not easy, I'm going senile! The other day he makes an effort, poor man, a surprise, brings me breakfast in bed, and seeing as I love surprises, you can imagine how happy I was. Coffee, croissants, apple juice, the works. Ah! It was a pretty picture, I can tell you. But the problem is, like most people, my brain's addled first thing in the morning. So I want to thank him and, I don't know why, I can't work out how my memory played hide-and-seek with my mouth, but instead of saying "Thank you, Arnaud!" – because my husband's called Arnaud – well, guess what, I say: "Thank you, Bertrand!" – when Bertrand's my ex-husband, for

120

heaven's sake. So I won't even begin telling you what a scene that caused. Luckily, I didn't drop any other clangers, I didn't throw Frédéric and Gilles, the first two, into the mix. And the icing on the cherry was me not saying sorry, because it's not my style, plus it wasn't such a big deal. I can be bloody-minded when it comes to that kind of thing, and I don't mind admitting it. I never say "I'm sorry from the bottom of my heart", because there'd be nothing left in my heart for later, for the stuff that actually matters . . .'

Then she acts out the dating agency. She tells me about her husband's oldest son – apparently he's this drop-dead-gorgeous twenty-five-year-old. She's sure I'd like him and he'd like me too. If I've got it right, he's a subtle cross between Brad Pitt and Bill Clinton. Josiane says she could introduce him to me. Why not? I could always give it a go. I've already wasted my time giving a chance to all the ASBOS Linda and Nawel insist on bringing me, so it can hardly get any worse. As for Tonislav: no news.

After that, Josiane goes back to work, and I write in my notepad.

This is the story of a girl who had to grow up too quickly and who is often sad. What keeps her going, despite her daily worries, is the fact that the tiniest hint of something positive, which most people wouldn't even notice, fills her with joy. She often dreams of another life and she hopes it will happen soon.

One day, in the middle of a long queue, she

meets a foreign violinist who she falls in love with, in fast-forward mode. This poor girl, who is a bit of a simpleton, clings to him like the girl in *Titanic* clutching her plank of wood in the icy water. She believes in their relationship, something that has never happened to her before, perhaps it is her turn at last to discover the raptures of love.

Alas no, just when she thinks she has reached nirvana, and allowed herself to open up her rusty heart, the violinist disappears without a trace. She is so heartbroken and sad that she can't even see the point in being heartbroken and sad any more and so she vows to forget him forever.

I told Auntie all about my story, inside out, back to front, in back-slang too. Given how well she knows me, she thought it was astonishing that I had fallen for him so quickly, and so hard. Normally, I faff around for months and months before cracking, and many lay down their weapons before the battle's over. The interested party needs to be very patient and determined to win a piece of my heart and my trust, or at least enough to start a relationship . . . And once started, generally speaking it never lasts long. Either the bloke runs off before I've even had time to learn his phone number by heart and dream up ridiculous nicknames for him, or I get out first because I'm bored of him already. So it's safe to say that Tonislav has beaten the record. European champion for 'speedy getaway', heavyweight category for 'mysterious dis-appearance' . . .

Truth is, there's this blinding feeling of rage inside me. It's totally out of character for me to cry myself to sleep at night because an illegal tramp from Eastern Europe hasn't called me back. It's nuts . . . They're all bastards, the whole lot of them, and like Linda said the other day, 'It's when you think you've found the exception to the rule that it's the biggest letdown of all.' In other words, you get caught out most when you're least expecting it.

Auntie Mariatou says I should give him a bit of time, but I've been hanging around for two weeks already. For someone who was supposed to call me the next day, that seems kind of long . . . Seeing as she always has an answer for everything, Auntie made a list of what might have happened to him, poor old Tonislav, like losing my number, or having an acci-dent or getting sick . . . Maybe he was a secret agent too, while we're at it. I'm fed up of making excuses for everybody. I don't make any for me. So why should I for anyone else?

So I cussed that bastard for all I was worth, using all the swear words I know, in several languages. I dissed him and his descendants, I prayed that seven future generations would be born eunuchs, with four eyes and seventeen fingers.

Auntie says I'm just making a big scene, that I'm not thinking about what I'm saying, because I'm not a bad girl at heart and I'm perfectly capable of giving people the benefit of the doubt.

If you ask me, he's not coming back. Not only that, but I'm bound to bump into him again one day at the immigration office. I've even thought about passing by, although my next appointment isn't due. I'm convinced that if I see him, he'll be scared shit-less, and he'll feel *this* ashamed, like so ashamed he'll have to hide. But then I tell myself there's no point thinking like that. I'll only end up looking even more ridiculous in his eyes. And if I do that, I'll have squashed my dignity once and for all, and given my pride a life sentence. It's the end of the road. Forget him. In fact, I promise never to talk about him again, I won't even let myself think about him. I've decided to blank him from my memory, like he never existed. There won't be any regrets, between Tonislav and me – just like between the Danone factory and those two hundred employees who got made redundant.

The Life of a Stray Dog

I'm starting to enjoy having a proper job.

The decision to hire me was based on totally unfair criteria, nothing to do with my skills. I got this position because I'm Nawel's friend, and she's my boss's favourite niece, plus I'm a fluent Arabic speaker, which is kind of useful around here. For once in my life someone's given me a leg-up, and I'm not complaining. Nawel's uncle, Uncle Abdou, is a really nice man, I like him a lot – although I call him Mr Kadri at the shop, because you shouldn't mix stuff up.

From now on, my job is selling shoes.

I spend my days hanging out with feet, and I hate that. Feet are such a turn-off. I see long ones, wide ones, strange ones, dirty ones, old ones, fat ones, slender ones, but I hardly ever get to see good-looking ones. Some totally stink. I've got this idea of taking photos of the most hideous ones and compiling an album with a Top Ten of Unbelievable Feet. There's even a business plan to go with it: the winner of the Ugliest Tootsies competition would receive a free pair of creps. Which all goes to prove I've got issues with feet, including my own, I think they're horrible now. I can't bring myself to look at them any more. Sometimes, when I get a customer to try on a shoe, I think about Cinderella and tell myself that if she'd had revolting feet, with dirty nails and blistered toes, the story would have ended differently. The Prince would have thrown the glass slipper in that grimy girl's face and run for his life.

So these days, I spend my life surrounded by shoeboxes and strangers' feet, but I've got my head strong. Uncle Abdou's shop is in this great location on the Boulevard de la Chapelle, bang in the middle of the crazy Barbès district. I love this area. As soon as I get a break, I walk around it. I've even developed a few local habits. I head over to Mr Yassine's for lunch, he's this old Algerian with a sandwich shop higher up the street. His halal toasted sandwiches are something else.

Afterwards, I go to this newspaper stand run by Kaïs and he's a bit odd, like he's not all there. What's really weird is he never finishes his sentences, but it's so natural with him that he gets away with it. I buy my newspaper and go for a coffee at the *tabac* opposite.

One day, I got it into my head that I wanted to find Slimane's famous café, the one the Boss had told me so much about. I was sure I'd recognise it straight up if I walked past it, because it was at the heart of so many of his stories and he'd described it in such detail . . . I combed the area, going round it several times, no luck. I ended up asking two old

Algerians sitting on a bench if they knew where I'd find Slimane and his place. One of them, in a checked cap, told me the café had been bought up several years back and turned into a Chinese restaurant. As for Slimane, from what the old man was saying, he'd lost his battle with cancer only a few months ago, and his children had decided to bury him back in the *bled* as that had always been their father's wish. I'd obviously touched on a subject close to their hearts, because both the old men launched into a big nostalgia trip.

'Slimane, may God keep his soul, *miskine*. You see, my brother, what awaits us, we'll end up the same way . . . After working here all our lives like stray dogs, they'll send us back over there dead, between the four wooden planks of a coffin.'

'Don't talk about such misfortune. God will provide and that is all, we decide nothing.'

'Yes, my brother. My only dream was to go back home. Every year, I used to say: next year; then I said: when I've retired; and then I put it off again saying: when the children have grown up. Now, they're grown up, thanks be to God, but they don't want to follow me. They say that they are French and their life is here.'

'What do you think you can offer them in the old country? There isn't even work for the children of the *châab*, and you think your *franssaouis* offspring will find any?'

'Well, they won't find work here either.'

Then one of them turned to me.

'Tell me, my daughter, why are you looking for Slimane? Are you a relative?'

'No, but my father knew him.'

'Who's your father?'

'Moustafa Galbi.'

'Moustafa Galbi . . . Galbi . . . Where's he from?'

'He's from Tlemcen.'

'So your father must be Galbi the Moustache?'

The two old men burst out laughing. And the one wearing the checked cap started coughing like an asthmatic sow. He was laughing so hard, at one point I thought: 'We're going to lose him.'

'My friend, I don't believe it! Do you remember him?'

'No one forgets Sam! That rascal, I never managed to take a single game of dominoes off him!'

'You know, my daughter, your father used to play in that café, he used to play the guitar, I remember . . .'

'Yes, he told me about that.'

'Well, your passing by this way is a funny sign. Tell your father he has greetings from Najib and Abdelhamid of Oran.'

'I'll tell him, inshallah.'

'And tell the old fool he can always come and see us, we often sit here.'

The old fool, as the gentleman affectionately referred to him, probably won't remember them at all, but I'll tell him about this meeting anyway. I said goodbye and then made my escape, because otherwise they would have talked to me for hours about an era I didn't know and can't really imagine. Seeing how emotional I get, I think I'd even have shed a tear or two in front of them. And then they'd have thought I was the one who was crazy.

And I guess I am, deep down, because I keep thinking I've seen that bastard Tonislav when I walk past the little Serbian bar on the other side of the street. My heart beats as loud as the *bendirs* of Tlemcen, and then, as I get nearer, I realise it's not him. The worst is, I feel so disappointed.

The Right to Dream

The thing I was dreading most has happened, Foued has been permanently excluded from college. It's not even like they were in two minds about it. They invited me to this rushed disciplinary hearing where they deliberated before reaching their decision but, if you ask me, it had already been taken.

Here are the facts: during his end-of-year interview with the teachers and the careers adviser, Foued explained he'd like to do sports studies, specialising in football, because that's been his passion since forever – he was six when he first played for an Ivry club. It's what he enjoys, and he wants to turn professional. And here's the guidance the careers counsellor thought fit to give him: 'There's no point dreaming, you're not being realistic. I won't take responsibility for sending you to some sports academy, not everybody can become a Zidane. You should train as an electrician or a mechanic instead. I think that's what would suit you best.'

End result: Foued, who's highly strung, let rip.

He stood up, started hurling all sorts of insults at her, including calling her a harlot, which amused his French teacher – a complete bastard if you ask me – because he thought it was ironic that Foued was able to use a fourteenth-century French word when he couldn't write a single sentence without making spelling mistakes. He remarked on this loudly, which made some of his colleagues chuckle. So there you go, no doubt he enjoyed putting my brother down when his whole future was at stake. Foued has been excluded from the educational system because his dream had already been written off.

I contacted Thomas, one of the youth workers who deals with the Uprising Estate, to ask for help finding my brother another college. He explained that at this stage in the year it wouldn't be easy, particularly given the file they've got on Foued. He said it'd be better for him to repeat the year and look for a place for next autumn. So we've suddenly got a bit of time on our hands. I asked Uncle Abdou to let me have a two-week holiday. So as to persuade him, I even said I'd go without holidays for twenty years if I could just have this fortnight. He understood how impor-tant these two weeks are for me and gave me the time off without haggling. I think now's the right moment. I've reserved three tickets on Air Algeria.

I had to tell my brother we were going. I think it came as a real surprise to him. He was doing the drying-up, and he broke a glass from our Nutella range. It saves money and it's practical, the way you can reuse those jars as glasses. We've also got a glass-ware service in the Maille mustard range, and another from Garnerth olive cocktails.

'But I don't speak Arabic proper,' Foued objected.

'Don't worry, most people in the *bled* understand French.'

'Are we going to stay for long?'

'No, not long. Two weeks, something like that.'

'What are we going to do about the Boss?'

'Well, he's coming with us. We're not going to leave him in the rubbish chute.'

'Does he know? Have you told him we're going back?'

'Yeah, I told him just now. Ask him, you'll see, it'll make you laugh.'

Here's us in the living room with the Boss, who's busy making paper hens out of the pages from *Télé 7 Jours*.

'Dad?'

'That's me. Who's asking?'

'Where are we going, Dad? Do you know?'

'Gambetta, Les Andalouses, Bel-Air . . . to Oran. Yes, I know.'

'We're going back to the *bled*, aren't we? And we're going back to the village too. Like I told you. D'you remember?'

'Yes. I'm fed up with the adverts on One. Always ads.'

'We're going with Foued. We're going to take the plane.'

'Daylight robbery! Nine hundred and thirty-four euros, return flights. We're not rich. Bunch of crooks . . . I could swim there. It's not far.'

Foued and me laugh. You never know what the Boss is going to say next.

I'm meeting Linda and Nawel. It's been a hot minute since I saw their faces; I've missed them. We're supposed to meet at Café Babylon in Ménilmontant, near the youth centre where Nawel works. She often goes to this bar with her colleagues, so she knows it well. She says it's nothing special to look at, but it's a great place.

I arrive first, and sure enough it doesn't look like much from the outside. I push open the door and instantly take back my first impressions, I love the atmosphere: soft lighting, warm colours and there's a Manu Chao song playing. All the right ingredients. I feel like I belong. Near to the bar, I notice this weird-looking guy, he's about forty and seems kind of eccentric, long legs, a sailor's cap, big blue eyes, the kind of eyes that have stories to tell. He sees me and calls out: 'Hello, princess! Welcome! Make yourself at home! What will it be?' I ask for a *café serré*.

'Why a *café serré*?'

He totally catches me off guard, this weirdo. It's the first time anyone's asked me to justify my order in a bar.

'Er . . . dunno. It's what I always drink, out of habit.'

'Habit is what kills us. I'm Jack. But people call me Jack the Weasel!'

'I'm Ahlème.'

It's like he wants to make me crazy.

'Welcome. I'm saying "welcome" because it's your first time here.'

'Yes, that's right. I'll have a tea then, for a change.'

He delivers my order to the barman like a tennis player serving.

'One tea!'

Then the barman, who's got a grin glued to his face, repeats it like he wants to remember it for the rest of his life. 'A tea! A tea!'

I like the way he smiles. Generally speaking, when I go into cafés in Paris, I reckon the waiters have this hidden slot somewhere on their body and you've got to insert a coin for a glimmer of a grin. And no, I'm not trying to be disgusting.

The Weasel comes back over to me with the tea, which he puts down on a beer mat showing Planet Earth.

'Thanks a lot, Jack.'

'You're very lucky, you get to drink your tea on top of the world.'

'Yes . . . I hadn't thought of it like that.'

'You must be waiting for someone you like a lot, I can tell.'

'I'm waiting for my friends!'

'Ah! I was right. If you'd had a meeting with a bailiff or an accountant, I'd have known that too.'

Patter over, the Weasel abandons me as suddenly as he struck-up our conversation, leaving me to medi-tate gently on top of the world. Shit, I spill a puddle of tea on Africa, that's not a nice thing to do, like they haven't got enough crap to deal with. For someone called Jack, it sounds to me like he's got a bit of an Algiers accent. But I'd never ask him where he comes from, even if I became a regular at the café, because you shouldn't ask that kind of thing. Take me, for instance, I don't like it when people ask me, so I wouldn't ask him either, first of all because Jack suits him and that's enough for me, and secondly . . . ah, no, there isn't any secondly.

Linda and Nawel finally show up at Café Babylon. They're dressed to kill and, as usual, they make this sensational entrance in a cloud of cigarette smoke mixed with their oh-so-sophisticated perfume, it's a springtime fragrance. They play the part of girls who know the place, kisses all round, popping behind the bar like they're totally at home, smiles left, right and centre. I'm really disappointed to see Linda's dyed her pretty brown curls; she's had these dried-up burnt-out peroxide highlights put in and they're butterz. What a waste. Worse: a crime against humanity. They both come over to me. I reckon they've missed me too, so there's warm hugs and kisses and I invite them to join me on the banquette at the back, same old.

'Have you noticed anything?'

'Your hair?'

'Yeah!' she says, enthusiastically.

'You talking about that piss-coloured blonde dye? The armed assault your hair's just suffered?'

'No! You're kidding me? You don't like it?'

'Too right!'

'See! I told you!' Nawel chips in.

'Why not? Don't you think it looks pretty?'

'Fuck me, Linda, you're a fool! You had the most beautiful hair in the world, and you go and dye it with poster paint to look like all the common dirty little slappers who buy their leopard-skin thongs from Clignancourt market on a Saturday morning.'

'Shit! That's harsh . . . I was picturing this blonde colour, somewhere between golden blonde and ash blonde, it'll be summer soon, that's why.'

'You're getting me vexed! And another thing, your hairdresser, can't you see she's flopped the colour? It's not golden or ash, it's . . . smoked, it's nicotine yellow.'

'OK, forget it. I'm really pissed off, I can see she's flopped it, I just wanted to kid myself it was nice, but hey, shit, I'm a bad actress, there you go . . . You're right, it's ova-butterz, I'll admit it. That bitch of a hairdresser round at Jean-Louis David's brainwashed me, I've been had, she managed to convince me it suited me like *this* well. *And* I left her a five-euro tip! Let's go back and rip off her face! I'm fuming now, that's it . . .'

At which point bad-girl Nawel bursts out laughing. Luckily, Linda isn't exactly oversensitive. Anything goes, between us girls. Seeing as we're not as bad as all that, we suggest she buys a Movida dye and we'll do it for her at home so she turns back into the dark and dusky brunette who used to start a riot every time she walked by, the girl who men dreamt about in broad daylight, the one who reminded people of the princess's tales in *A Thousand and One Nights.*

So maybe I'm exaggerating, but it's just to emphasise that she's much prettier as a brunette.

Changing the subject, Linda tells us the latest gossip, still warm and wrapped in gold paper. The kind of thing you should tell the scriptwriters on the most successful American soaps. They'd know what to do with it, that's for sure.

A few days back, Magalie, her boss at Body Boom, decided to go home early as a nice surprise for her husband's birthday. She asked Linda and the other beauticians to manage the salon without her and, exceptionally, to lock up. Of course, like all stories that start with 'she decided to go back home early as a nice surprise for her husband . . .', you've guessed it already, there's a horrible ending. So poor Magalie heads for home, doing everything she can to make it a successful surprise: she takes a different route from usual, tries to be discreet, climbs the stairs without making any noise, etc, etc. All these precautions are totally stupid because the husband in question isn't even meant to be there . . . You've got to imagine how it is when Linda tells the story, she sets the whole scene, down to the tiniest detail. I prefer leaving that stuff out, because it doesn't make the fall any tastier.

Magalie's on top of the world as she goes into the dining room to lay the magnificent table, for a romantic candlelit dinner with her darling husband. But to her astonishment, there on the sofa they'd bought together from the Swedish furniture giant, was her fat pig of a husband in the arms of a seventeen-year-old Chinese guy. From what I remember, the story ended with her having an epileptic fit, or strangling the Chinese guy . . . or maybe it was the Chinese guy who strangled her . . . I can't remember any more.

After that, it's Nawel's turn to strangle me, with no warning or anything. Without meaning to, she kills me. She always makes sure she's current with everything going on in the world, unlike Linda who's more into what you might call local news. So on the phone, Nawel had mentioned this article she'd read a few days ago, it's all about a new form of deportation for illegal immigrants. In front of me, she gets the newspaper out of her bag and starts reading it out loud.

'You'll see, it's bare crazy. *"The man, aged twenty-seven, presented himself in the morning at the immigration office in Val-de-Marne, following a petty summons. Suspecting nothing, he arrived clutching the promise of employment that would enable him to obtain the elusive ten-year residency permit. He was shown a room where he was meant to wait for an administrative officer, but to his astonishment two police officers came to get him. Destination: the local detention centre. And then the first plane for Belgrade –"'*

I grab the newspaper out of Nawel's hands. The heading is: 'When the Immigration Authorities Lie in Ambush'.

'Whoa, take it easy –'

139

'Let me see! Let me see!'

Straight up, I spot the passage I've been dreading.

... *The Home Office Minister denies 'having set traps for anybody'. The case of Tonislav Jogovic, however, is not unique. According to the organisation 'Papers for All', his case will be the thirteenth of its kind since the decree in February.*

The Other Side

The first step on Algerian soil is difficult, my body tenses. I'm wearing a dress that twirls and, seeing as it's a bit windy, I hold it down. The sun here in the *bled* shames my white legs, which I never expose.

The smell is instantly familiar, the perfume of the earth, the warm air hitting your face. And still that letter missing from above the entrance: AÉRO ORT ORAN-ES-SENIA.

The mustachioed customs officer is too thorough searching the bags, he turns all my stuff upside down after it took me hours to organise, and he's giving me this dodgy look. No doubt about it, it's the word *bakchich* I'm seeing in his eyes. Fat chance. I'd rather die in this airport than grease the goose of corruption. So, the show goes on, he's really dragging it out as he watches us in the hope we'll pull a big note out of our pockets. Best-case scenario: 'hard currency' in euros; at worst, a fistful of two-hundred dinar notes. He makes no secret of the kick he gets from keeping us waiting, the way he's rummaging around you'd think the eighteen times we've been through customs and automatic doors since Paris-Orly wasn't enough. Determined to get the result he wants, the customs officer calls over one of his female colleagues for a 'very-fication'. Actually, he just gives her the nod and she gets it straight away. So, this short woman arrives with purpose in her stride, and Moustache has a word in her ear – from what I'm seeing, they want to play it on the down-low. This woman's got a giant head that looks like it's tucked right in to her body. No neck, she looks like the tortoise in that *Big Turtle* cartoon that used to be on Channel 5 when we were kids. She talks to me in a deep voice: she would like to know what those objects are that I've wrapped in newspaper. I explain to Big Turtle that they're boxes of capsules for my grandmother who's sick. She wants to know more, so I tell her she can open them if she likes. What's she thinking? That I'm bringing Ecstasy tablets back to my granny in the *bled*? She prods the boxes through the paper, chewing her gum in this tacky way, then I spot her stopping over a piece of newspaper. She's completely still for a few minutes. And get this, she's busy reading, like we've got nothing better to do. We wait some more . . . What on earth is she doing?

'What date's this newspaper? Is that today's horo-scope?'

Then she goes back to her post, dissatisfied. The predictions can't have been good.

The Boss is blasted by the heat, even more phased than usual. I've given him a booklet on security procedures that I jacked from the plane, to fan himself with. Foued seems totally out of his depth. He's looking around everywhere, like a lost child in a shopping centre. The guy in uniform carries on but then, seeing he's not having any luck with trying to break us, he ends up closing the bags and marking them with a small cross in white chalk, which means everything's OK. He lets us go reluctantly, like a fisherman letting a big salmon slip away. We pick up our luggage and make for the exit. I spot him giving us one last evil look, as he twizzles his moustache between his thumb and index finger. I wonder what he's thinking, probably: 'Immigrants, pah! Stingy bastards! When you think of all that money they earn in France . . .'

In front of the arrivals door, there are people waiting under the palm trees. The sun hits the windscreens and the backs of the taxi drivers' heads, as they poach the travellers from every side. They shout out their destinations, the small villages they'll be passing through. Passengers clamber into the vehicles, chucking the cases into the boot and *vroom*, off they screech, pulling out like they're in some American car chase.

We're waiting for our cousin Youssef. I'm not even sure I'll recognise him, but he's bound to recognise us.

For some minutes now, Foued's ready to follow every taxi driver who comes over to us and calls the Boss '*aâmi*', because he thinks this must be the cousin we're waiting for. So I explain it's just a polite form of address and that all the guys who'll call him '*khoyya*' over here aren't necessarily his brothers. It's a bit like his crew back on the estate when they call each other cuz or bredrin.

Youssef finally shows up. It's an emotional reunion but a bit odd because, basically, it's with someone I don't know. Or barely. He's a man now, worry has made him old before his time, and apart from that malicious sparkle in his eyes, the impish kid I used to play forbidden games with has disappeared. We get into the taxi and our cousin tries to make conversation with the Boss. It's not easy, but he sticks with it. I'd warned him, explained all about it so he wouldn't be too shocked by the change. In fact, I warned them all about Dad being sick. They're used to it with Uncle Kader, who's been like that since he got out of the army – I wonder what they did to him over there? If Aunt Hanan's letters are anything to go by, it was harsh. Something snapped inside him. Apparently, he pisses himself in the middle of the market, and sometimes he takes all his clothes off in the street and tries to run off. Youssef asks us questions, what we're up to, he wants to know about our lives. I tell him I work, but he seems disappointed when I tell him what my job is. As for Foued, he lies, says he goes to school and that he's studying hard. He gulps before lying: it looks like we have the same technique. He avoids meeting my gaze when he does it. Maybe he's frightened I'll show him up, bring big shame on him in front of a *blédard*, as he calls them.

'Your sister wrote in the letter you're still playing *boleta*, Foued.'

'Yeah, no big deal.'

'Why don't you ever write any letters?'

'Coz I'm not so good at French.'

'And what about me? I'm worse than you, but I still write. You're a slacker, you little *Franssaoui* . . .'

One to the *blédard*, I think to myself.

It's too hot in this place, the beads of sweat are trickling down my forehead. The air is dry and, through the open window, the dust flies into my eyes. The taxi man drives like a lunatic and I'm about to spend a fortnight with people I haven't seen for over ten years and who I don't even know that well.

The day before we left for Algeria, I went to say goodbye to Auntie Mariatou. I told her some of my worries about the trip ahead. I was so scared of not having anything in common with my relatives any more, I was afraid of France having stamped its mark on me so I'd feel even more of a foreigner over there. She gave me one of her juicy sayings that I packed in my luggage: '*Even if a plank of wood lies in the river a hundred years, it will never be a caiman.*'

It's just the way I'd imagined it, the whole village is looking out for us, there's a crowd gathered in front of the house. I don't know who all these people are waiting to see me, all these expectant faces, I wonder what I'm going to say to them. I'm as disorientated as a fledgling who's lost its nest.

The taxi parks in a cloud of dust, I catch sight of the family place, Dar Mounia, and something tugs at my heart. It takes my breath away, everything's happening so quickly. This is where I grew up, and the first thing I notice is how small everything is. My memory is right there in front of me, but scaled down. We get out of the car and, while Foued and cuz Youssef get the suitcases out of the boot, the Boss decides to make a dramatic entrance. I don't know what's got into him but he bounces out of the car and starts shouting with joy, raising his arms, clapping and whistling. What's even crazier is the crowd follows the vibe, like the audience at the start of an NTM concert, back in the day.

'*Vive l'Algérie!* The Algerian people are free! We've won! Algeria is ours! *Istiqlal! Istiqlal!*'

People are laughing, and children are running around us. They're trying to cling on to us, our clothes and arms. It's insane. They start shouting: 'The immigrants! The immigrants! So where's Jacques Chirac?'

Then I recognise a few familiar faces coming our way. The aunts, uncles and cousins fling themselves at us, they kiss us, give us these great heart-felt hugs. We're welcomed with this mad euphoria, we're carried on a wave of shouts and *yu-yus*, the village is on holiday because a little piece of France is visiting it. The '*salaams*' and the '*labès*' start up now. I feel like a whole week goes by between our arrival and the moment we finally enter the house.

Slowly but surely, the details are coming back to me. I find my secret corner. I used to think you could see all of Algeria here. The wire fence, where I used to spy on passers-by so I could make up stories about them, has been replaced by a low stone wall. My beautiful orange tree has disappeared. They've cut it down and replaced it with a water pump and big earthenware sinks for doing the laundry. Apart from that, Dar Mounia hasn't really changed.

My grandmother has aged, she's sick. She lost all her teeth, so she can only eat soup and puréed vegetables now. She spends her time sleeping because she gets tired so quickly. The poor old lady ova-LIKES Foued. He's got a special place in her heart because she was the one who rocked him to sleep, whispering traditional songs in his ear, and she got to choose his name. Trouble is he avoids her, the little shit, because I think she scares him. 'She freaks me out, man, with those drawings on her face, plus her breath stinks! She's like the serial killer in *Saw*!' He's talking about the tribal tattoos she has on her forehead and chin. They don't do that kind of stuff so much now, but from what I'm hearing it was a horrendous ordeal back in the day. A few old women from the village were in charge, with their hot needles, and those old bags weren't much of a laugh, we're talking proper hyenas. No matter how hard you struggled to escape, to wrestle yourself free, there was no way out, they held your head tight. My grandmother told me how, as a little girl, my mum ran away to hide in the forest, when they wanted to do it to her. She laughed as she was telling the story, opening her empty mouth wide.

My memory of Aunt Hanan was reasonably accurate. She's a walking melodrama, she cries the whole time, about anything and everything. When I see her starting to scrunch her eyebrows and twist her lips, I think: 'Oh, shit! Here we go again!' Luckily, she hasn't seen *Titanic*.

She talks to me a lot about how it was when I used to live here. She makes me look at these old Polaroids, she even shows me where I used to sleep . . . It's like she wants to give me back all the things I might have lost along the way. She tells me that France snatched me from the arms of my country, the way a child is snatched from its mother. And there you go, no sooner has she said it than she scrunches her eyebrows and her lips start to quiver . . . And she's got a few more magic formulas where that one came from. Aunt Hanan could make a truck driver weep.

I spend my days listening to people, and trying to remember where I come from. I'm finding it hard to admit, but this isn't my place any more either.

My young girl cousins only have one word – 'marriage' – on their lips. They're getting their trousseaus ready and, at Foued's age, they're already proper women. Their life is embroidered into their straw rugs as surely as mine is carved into the concrete of the tower blocks in Ivry. Every afternoon they fantasise about another life, far away and out of reach, as they watch the orange-flower-water-scented Mexican soap, badly dubbed into Arabic – with all the 'hot' scenes missing, censored, because they're allowed to dream, but not too much. This slush is on every afternoon at one o'clock. So, in the village, life stops at one o'clock. And after the soap, it's siesta time.

Which is exactly when poor Foued loses it.

'Fuck, it's dead here, I wanna go outside, man . . .'

'But nobody's outside now.'

'What kind of *bled* is this where everyone sleeps?'

'It's too hot outside at this time of day. D'you think you're in France or what? If you go outside now, you'll pass out, you'll see. The sun'll mash your brain.'

The 'cousins', the ones who live in France and only come back to the *bled* for the holidays, don't talk about anything except their new country. It's like they're talking about this new girlfriend: sometimes she holds out her arms to them, sometimes she kicks them away. They tell these stories, stories they've heard from guys who slipped through the net, and they big them up, so they don't have to admit to being broke or a failure. They never let on to their families that they're working on the black, washing up in rank Chinese restaurants and sleeping in tiny grimy maids' rooms. They make it all sound rosy, because they're ashamed, but they still reckon it's better than coming back for good.

Cousin Youssef'll never know what France is really like. He told me half the population here's under twenty-five and powerless, so they don't know what to do with their dreams.

I'd like to tell them that over there, in France, it's not what they think, and they'll never get the truth through that distorting window people call television. They hack into French channels to watch the TF1 summer soaps, but *they* don't show reality. Young people round here say the satellite dishes on Oran's residential blocks are the city's ears, straining towards the north, ready to hear everything. But those ears are blocked.

I can't bring myself to tell them all that, I don't want to seem like Mrs Know-It-All. These people have experienced civil war, hunger and terror, and even if France isn't what they think it is, we're not so badly off over there, at the end of the day it's probably worse here.

After a bout of the diarrhoea, which is traditional for the first three days in the *bled*, Foued managed to click with the neighbours. The kids round here have already nicknamed him the 'Im'grant'. They spend their days together in the area, cotchin' in front of the *hanout*. His new bredrin from the endz are the kids from the *bled*, guys who find a way to get by, for real; they sell plastic bags, peanuts and single cigarettes in the street, they spend days rummaging around in bins looking for a miracle or a pair of shoes. Even though we're not staying here for very long, I hope Foued will recognise that money isn't so easy to get hold of, that these kids who walk about with fake 'Mike' flip-flops, with dirty aching feet, who get blasted by adults all day long, including their parents in the evening when they haven't earned enough dinars, these kids suffer but they keep their heads strong and mostly they don't complain. I hope that seeing what life's like here will make him think.

Today, we're going to the town, first to the seafront and then to the cemetery where Mum is buried. The Boss'll join us after the brothers Djamel and Aïssa have driven him to the *marabouts* in the neighbouring village to do what they call a *ziara* here, a sort of 'taking the spell off'. It's the same ritual as for curing madness, a curse, or treating disturbed children. We'll see what happens, it can't make it any worse.

While everyone's getting ready, I stand under the olive tree opposite the house. I listen to Algeria, I breathe in its smells and I write it all down in my notepad.

I even write about the little wooden comb that my aunts smooth my hair down with. I write about Isis, the brand that's got a monopoly here on washing powder, as well as shampoos, soap, washing-up liquid, toothpaste and sanitary towels . . .

I write about the big party on the first evening that was organised in our honour, the sheep that had its throat slit before being roasted on a spit, all the new faces I've had to memorise in such a short time.

I write about my cousin Khadra who is glued to me all day long, and never stops complimenting me on the Agnès B cardigan I'm wearing. She touches it, says she'd like one the same, that she's looked for one everywhere in the clothes shops in Oran, that she thinks it feels so soft, new . . . She's probably hoping I'll take it off and give it to her, but it was a birthday present from Linda and Nawel. She applies all this psychological pressure, my cousin Khadra. Foued was the first to suss her out, and he doesn't hold back from giving me warnings.

'She'll suck you dry, that one, I've never seen it

that bad, it's a jumper, *wesh*, it's like she's never seen a jumper before.'

'It's not just any old jumper, it's my Agnès B jumper.'

'Yeah, nice one . . . So the cuz, she knows her labels, innit, she's got a nose for it.'

I don't forget to write down the stuff that makes Foued laugh, in my notebook. His big thing is talking in French in front of the cousins who don't get a word, poor things, and most of all he drives them crazy by teaching them these slang words. So all of a sudden, I hear Aunt Norah's little kids playing in the courtyard singing at the top of their voices: 'Fuck the Fidz, innit! Fuck the Fidz!'

And I write about the cousin from Aïn Temouchent who asked for my hand in marriage after I'd been here three days. He's called Bilel, and he's the village sex symbol, a 'guy-lite' as Foued puts it. He's got blue eyes and they're his USP. All the wifeys in this *bled* want him as a husband just for his blue eyes. He comes to Dar Mounia every day to see me, thinks he's *it*, fluttering his eyes at me. He thinks he's making this big impression on me, but he's forgetting I live in France, and all I have to do is catch the Métro to see them, blue eyes I mean. If he goes on showing off like this, God will punish him for his arrogance, and one morning, with no idea what's going on, he'll wake up with brown eyes. And they'll be the commonest brown in the world. That'll teach him.

People have even talked to me about the vague 'marriage of convenience' proposals bandied around with my name on them. Guys offering totally incredible sums of money to marry a *Cif,* with the bids rising to seven thousand euros. What I want to know is where do they find all this dough? Plus it's scary to see what they're prepared to pay for life on the other side.

The sardine seller drives past on his moped. The noise from his engine makes me lose my concentration. He's driving like a slacker, he should do a spot of training with Speed Pizza – if the order isn't delivered within half an hour, the pizza's on the house, so it's in the driver's interests to get a move on. It's funny how life happens in slow motion here. Even though we haven't been here for very long, hectic Paris already seems a long way away. I can tell my little brother's glad to be here, but I hope he also understands his life isn't in the *bled* and he's got to calm down when we get back, because these stories about immigrants getting deported are worrying me more and more. I think about it all the time, even here. I keep going back over Tonislav's story, and every day I realise how those bastards trashed my love story and set fire to that poor guy's straw dreams. And now they think they're going to take my little brother away from me?

At last we leave for the post office, in town. We walk into this huge room, lined with rows of payphones, suffocating in an infernal hubbub, drowning in a whirlpool of djellabas and *hayeks*. All I want to do is call Auntie Mariatou to let her know we're fine and find out how the little ones are doing.

So we head over to the VIP corner, the one reserved for international calls, and that's where I see what happens to the ones who get sent over here, spirited away to serve out their second sentence. They've got the same look in their eyes as my brothers whose paths I cross early in the morning at the Gare Saint-Lazare, the ones who are cold and who walk with their heads down. Rammed around the phone booths, these guys, who are as French as Foued or me, hold the receiver nervously, keeping a worried eye on the counter. Sometimes they want to spin it out a bit longer, so they grope around at the bottom of their pockets for one last coin – they always say it's the last one . . . They call their mother, their friends, maybe their girlfriend, they try to talk loudly to cover the noise, basically they're just trying talk, end of. I explain all this to Foued; he watches them, and I think he's as shocked as I am. When we get back into Uncle Mohamed's car, nobody says a word. We're silent all the way to the cemetery.

The rusty gate is wide open. What hits me first is how white this place is, and how far it stretches. It's really upsetting.

But most frightening of all are the dates of birth, too recent, all these rows of graves, these five-point stars directed towards the east. It's hard to accept, but there are children under all this. That's when I realise how me and Foued, we could have been buried here too. So easily. There were two hundred deaths that night, so two more . . .

The Boss is crouching down in front of the tomb, silent, stroking the white stone with his fingertips. From time to time, he lets out a sigh, it's like he understands everything, he knows. I'm convinced that at this moment in time, he's found his head again.

Foued stays standing, eyes lowered. I can hear him sniffing but I don't dare look at him to find out if he's crying.

And me, I'm sitting on the red earth, the palms of my hands on the ground, like I want it to give me strength, the courage to go away again and deal with life.

We say a prayer for her, for those who lie here and also for those who mourn them, for us, for the ones from over there. We'll make a *sadaqa* in her memory this afternoon, at the mosque.

Time doesn't rattle by in the same way in Algeria, the day of our departure sneaks up on us. I promise to come back very soon, so as not to forget. There's something in this *bled* I'll never find anywhere else. The atmosphere is peculiar, the smell too and above all it's hot, maybe too hot. After all, it's just a question of climate: the heat of Algeria has anaesthetised me.

Foued wants to stay on a few more days with the Boss. We do a deal on the tickets to postpone their return. As for me, I've got to go back because Uncle Abdou is ready and waiting for me at the shop.

Truce

Technically I'm KO, all night long I've pulped my body on the dance floor at Club Tropical, like I'm on fire, thanks to the talents of DJ Patrick-Romauld. I'm making the most of being on my own. I've still got a week of freedom before Foued and the Boss get back. I've got the flat to myself.

Last night, with Linda and Nawel, we let our hair down big time. We managed to shake off their guys, Issam and Mouss. It was easy, there was a match on telly.

We spent the evening with these Brazilian dancers, Coco, Miguel and Roberto. They were looking this *cris*. Three fit guys who were heavy dancers. They taught us two or three new steps and bought us two or three fruit cocktails. Coco, the most handsome of the three, followed me round all evening and I can't say I minded. We were joined at the hip, we danced, we sweated. I thought I'd died and gone to heaven.

Around four, Coco and me decided to leave Club Tropical. The others stayed on. In the cloakroom, while we were picking up our stuff, the girls were giving me the thumbs up and winking at me from a way off. It was embarrassing.

Coco's telling me about another party not far away. I think he's on a high, this guy, he's up for keeping going all night. We get into his Golf and it's like it's all been set up: cream leather seats, Marvin Gaye CD in the car stereo, and the smooth driving . . . This is doing things Coco-style. As we're driving along, he even puts his hand on my knee, smiles at me, asks me in his mellow voice if I'm doing OK.

We finally arrive. He parks the wib and gives me a gentle kiss. I can see the queue from here. There must be a hundred people. The last thing I feel like doing is queuing up. And even after all that waiting, there's no guarantee you'll get in. Plus, my feet hurt, I'm wearing these shoes from the shop. I realise I'm spending my days selling shoddy shoes. Bottom line is, Uncle Abdou's a crook.

As I get out of Coco's car, I can hear the birds. I hate hearing birds at dawn.

He gives me a wave and heads off. It's nice of him to drop me off like that. He looked disappointed I wasn't going to the party with him. He's promised to call me tomorrow, but if he doesn't, it's no big deal. Like Auntie often says: 'You've got to kiss a lot of frogs before you find your Prince.'

I head over to the queue. Always the same tired faces. These weary people. These foreigners who come at dawn for a ticket.

It's six o'clock in the morning and I'm in front of the immigration office.

For my family.
My father, Abdelhamid Guène.
My mother, Khadra Kadri.
My sister, Mounia Guène.
My brother, Mohammed Guène.
May you be proud of me.
I love you.

For all those who have supported and encouraged me.
For Les Courtillières, respect.
For my friends, thank you.
For those in prison, keep the hope alive.
For Algeria.
For all the crazies in the endz, here and over there.
For those who dream.

The translator would like to thank slangsta Cleo Soazandry, ex-editor of *Live Magazine*, Brixton.

And Sophie Moreau of the French Book Office, London.

Glossary of French Terms and Places

BAC Police Anti-Criminality Brigade.

Baron Pierre de Coubertin revived the modern Olympic Games, President of the IOC from 1896-1924.

bled originally an Arabic word for a plot of land or the interior of North Africa, this was adopted into metropolitan French to refer to a godforsaken place or village in the middle of nowhere. For North Africans living in France today, it refers to their homeland or mother country and, by extension, the country someone comes from. In the urban French slang of the second generation Maghrebi community, a *blédard* is someone who still lives back in the *bled*, or else a new arrival from the *bled*; the tone tends to be pejorative.

café serré espresso with half the normal amount of water.

Château D'Eau West African quarter of Paris, just north of *Barbès* and *La Goutte D'Or*, which forms the North African quarter.

cif someone holding a French Identity Card (*carte d'identité française*).

Claude François Egyptian-born King of Kitsch, of Pied Noir origin, whose song 'Belles, Belles, Belles' was voted by the French as their favourite song ever. He was tragically electrocuted in his bath in 1978, aged thirty-nine.

CPE (*contrat de premier embauche*) employment contract for first-jobbers. The student demonstrations Ahlème refers to in 'No Such Thing as Random' were against the CPE, and took place in March 2006. The government was trying to make the work

161

market open to taking on new labour at low risk. Students protested the new contract didn't provide them with enough security, and got the government to overturn its decision.

Diam's real name Mélanie Georgiades, a French-language rap artist of French and Greek Cypriot origin born in 1980. Diam's is an outspoken opponent of Jean-Marie and Marine Le Pen, as well as of French President Nicolas Sarkozy. She won the MTV Europe Music Awards 2006 for Best French Act and her album *Dans Ma Bulle* (*Inside my Bubble*) literally went 'diamond' (1 million copies sold).

double peine 'double penalty'. The controversial French system of deporting 'immigrants' who have served prison sentences in France. Under article 8 of the European Court of Human Rights ('the right to respect for private life') it is prohibited to deport somebody who has lived in a country for a number of years and has strong family links there. *Peine* can refer to sorrow as well as penalty, so the phrase technically means 'twice the misery' as well as 'double punishment'. Bertrand Tavernier's 2001 film *Vies Brisées* (*Broken Lives*) followed ten North Africans who faced the *double peine* and went on hunger strike in Lyon in 1998.

FAJ fund for young Parisians aged 18–24 who are in difficulty and looking to begin a professional placement and address their own integration.

Franky Vincent 'Zouk Love' crooner from Guadeloupe.

gadjo	'outsider' in Romany, referring to a male non-Roma, as in Tony Gatlif's film *Gadjo Dilo* (crazy outsider).
Ladji-Doucouré	French athlete of Malian-Senegalese descent who was a football player and decathlete before specialising in hurdling. Born in 1983 in Juvisy-sur-Orge, a suburb south of Paris, he won the 2005 World Athletic Championships 110 metres hurdles.
Leclerc	chain of French supermarkets and 'hypermarkets'.
Les Guignols d'Abidjan	comedy series from the Ivory Coast, performed by a francophone theatrical troupe from Abidjan.
Navarro	long-running detective series screened on France's main channel, TF1, from 1989–2007.
Navigo	public transport 'touch' pass in Paris, the equivalent of London's Oyster card.
Patrick Sabatier	housewives' favourite TV presenter from the 80s.
Pierre Bellemare	radio and TV presenter and writer, specialising in dramatic real life stories
PMU	government-regulated network of horse-racing betting counters run from bars displaying the PMU sign.
O Puberté j'écris ton nom	a playful variant on Paul Eluard's poem *Liberté* in which every verse ends with the refrain 'I write your name'.
RATP	(*régie autonome des transports Parisiens*) Paris Public Transport System.
RER	(*réseau express régional*) fast regional train connecting the *banlieue* or suburbs with the city centre.

Tati	cut-price retail chain for clothes and homeware.
TGV	*(train à grande vitesse)* high speed train.
Zizou	an affectionate nickname for French-Algerian football legend Zinedine Zidane.

Glossary of Algerian Arabic Terms and Places

aâmi	uncle.
aïn	casting the evil eye.
Aïn Temouchent	a town in north-western Algeria, founded in 1851 with the arrival of Spanish immigrants, it is on the site of Roman and Arab settlements.
Les Andalouses	a beach and village west of Oran. Brigadier General Theodore Roosevelt came ashore here on 8th November 1942 during 'Operation Torch', the joint invasion of North Africa by British and American troops. Oran fell to the Allies two days later.
bakchich	bribe.
baraka	derived from the Islamic word for knee, this refers to the rapture of a kneeling worshipper, designating the spiritual wisdom and blessing transmitted from God. More generally it means blessing or good luck.
Bel Air	a residential district of the cosmopolitan Algerian city of Oran, now rundown. The 1962 stand-off between the OAS (Secret Armed Organisation, a clandestine far-right movement responsible for terror attacks in France and

Algeria in the early 60s) and the 'barbouzes' (men from the French intelligence services intending to infiltrate OAS operations) was first apparent here.

belâani	a show.
bendir	hand-held North African drum that looks like a tambourine, but without the metal disks.
boleta	football, in the Algerian dialect.
châab	people. (Hence the world music term *châabi music* means music of the people.)
chétane	devil.
Dar Mounia	Mounia's house (Ahlème's mother's home).
Eid-el-Kebir	'The Big Festival' is also known as *Eid al Adha*, meaning 'Festival of Sacrifice' or 'Feast of the Sheep'.
djelleba	loose-fitting garment worn to cover clothes. This traditional North African hooded cloak or coat is typically woollen.
Franssaouis	French.
Gambetta	one of the more luxurious districts of Oran, developed by the French in the 1930s.
gandoura	a light dress worn in the house.
habs	prison.
hammam	bathhouse. Together with the mosque, this is an essential feature of an Islamic city.
hanout	shop.
hayek	traditional costume comprising a piece of bright-coloured cloth which women wind around themselves.

Insh'Allah	God willing.
istiqlal	Independence.
kabyle	term more commonly used in the Maghreb for 'Berber', referring to the regions of the Great Kabylie in the Djurdjura Mountains and the Little Kabylie around the Gulf of Bejaïa. The origin of the word 'Berber' is a bastardisation of the Roman word for barbarian.
khoyya	'my brother'.
labès	fine or good.
labès elhamdulillah	fine, thanks be to God.
marabout	witch doctor.
merguez	hallal spicy North African sausage made from lamb or beef, as distinct from the Spanish *chorizo*, which is made of pork.
miskina	poor girl or woman.
miskine	poor boy or man.
naâl chétane	a curse on the devil!
Sadaqa	offering.
Salam	peace. (After the greetings of 'peace' (*salam*), the typical response when asked how you are in Maghrebi Arabic is *labès elhamdulillah*.)
Sidi-bel-Abbes	a provincial capital in the Atlas Mountains of Western Algeria.
starfoullah!	May God preserve us!
wesh?	informal greeting equivalent to *wassup? Wesh Wesh, Qu'est-ce Qui Se Passe?* – was a 2002 film about the impact of the 'double penalty' by French/Algerian film-maker Rabah Ameur-Zaimeche.

yu-yu	ululating or making the 'yu-yu' euphoric wailing noise traditionally voiced by women at weddings.

West African References

Bambara	a language spoken in Mali by approximately six million people. Also known as *Bamanankan* within the language itself.
boubou	traditional West African dress.
kou yinkaranto!	'those idiots' in Soninké.
Soninké	Mande language spoken by the Soninké people of West Africa, who are from Mali, Senegal, the Ivory Coast, the Gambia, Mauritania, Guinea-Bissau and Guinea.
toubab	slang for 'white person', from the Senegalese Wolof language (Doria in *Just Like Tomorrow* riffs on different tags for a white person including 'asprin' and 'camembert').

Glossary of British Slang

ali!	(pronounced like 'ally', with the stress on the second syllable) is similar to 'innit'. Call and response: 'Ali!' – 'Atru!'
bare	very.
bare haps	very happy.
bare peeps	lots of people.
butterz	ugly.
creps	trainers.

167

cris garms	smart clothes.
dry	boring.
down low	on the sly.
feds	police.
5-0's	police.
to jack	to steal.
Jimmie	black hip-hop slang for penis.
J.O.B.	job.
LOL	laugh out loud (MSN messaging).
long	boring.
man dems	men.
ova	very.
ova-wack	rubbish.
pigs	police.
po-pos	police.
wasteman	loser.
wib	car.

Translator's Note on the Slang

The French title is *Du Rêve pour les Oufs*, which means 'Dreams for the Crazies' (*ouf* is the backslang of *fou* or 'mad person'). I discussed the title with Faïza and slangsta Cleo Soazandry – both were keen to emphasise the importance of dreams and aspiration over the slur of being a 'crazy', particularly given that society has condemned those on the margins *not to dream*. We wanted to capture the playful sound and raw urgency of the original title, while conveying that sense of lifting the lid on the ghetto, AKA a person's 'area' or 'endz'. *Dreams from the Endz* did just this.

Like Doria, the heroine of Faïza Guène's first novel, *Just Like Tomorrow*, Ahlème peppers her language with choice words from French *Verlan* or 'backslang'. This involves splicing and reversing words so that, for example, the French term *à l'envers* (meaning backwards, upside down or the wrong side up) becomes *verlan*. *Verlan* is the playful and defiant language of France's high-rise suburbs with their large immigrant communities. Although there is an improvised aspect to this wordplay, it is also systematic enough for words to filter on through to the mainstream. This explains why *beur*, which is the backslang for *arabe* (used to refer to a second or third generation French national of North African origin) has been flipped again by those deft beat-boxers who are ahead of the game to form *rebeu*. Incidentally, *beur* is now viewed as a politically correct and non-inflammatory term.

We do have examples of backslang in English, but there is no direct equivalent of *Verlan*. Where possible I have tried to find parallels and resonances in contemporary British urban slang, with the wide range of linguistic influences and ethnicities this draws on. In Britain as in France, the slang keeps moving of course. On the rise is 'Ali!' (pronounced like 'ally', with the stress on the second syllable), which is similar to 'innit', and works with the call and response: 'Ali!' – 'Atrue!' (A lie! A true!). The one word I regret not weaving in is 'showa', which has replaced 'bling'.

At twenty-four Ahlème is ten years older than Doria, so her language is more mature and wide-ranging. There is less overt teenage slang (such as 'oh my days!' to register shock or wonder, or 'bare' and 'ova', both meaning 'very'), though Ahlème can lapse into this register too with her childhood friends. Where the tone is loudly 'yoof', it is likely to be in the mouth of her disgruntled and disenfranchised younger brother Foued, with his refrain of ''low it, man!' for 'leave me alone' or 'back off'. The range of vocabulary maps Ahlème's own journeys. From the Arabic-influenced backslang of the *banlieue*, to the mainstream French of that 'other' Paris that exists inside the *périphérique* (ring-road) where Ahlème and Auntie Mariatou work. Or from the West African, Romany, East European and Turkish composition of the queues outside the immigration office, via the French Caribbean of Club Tropical, to the Maghrebi Arabic of Ahlème's home country, Algeria.

Faïza was writing *Dreams from the Endz* at the time of the Paris riots in November 2005. It is striking that while these sparked strong reactions in her own neighbourhood, she doesn't reference Sarkozy's notorious dubbing of the rioters as *racaille* ('scum' or 'vermin'). Instead, through such characters as Foued and Tonislav, she broadens the debate out into the root causes of the unrest. In the light of this, the title is all the more poignant – how can society (back in the *bled*, as well as in the troubled *banlieue*) give the next generation something to dream rather than riot about?